The
UNFORGIVEN

ANNE SCHRAFF

SADDLEBACK
EDUCATIONAL PUBLISHING

URBAN UNDERGROUND

SADDLEBACK
EDUCATIONAL PUBLISHING
www.sdlback.com

ISBN-13: 978-1-61651-586-7
ISBN-10: 1-61651-586-4
eBook: 978-1-61247-232-4

Printed in Guangzhou, China
0411/04-56-11

16 15 14 13 12   1 2 3 4 5

CHAPTER ONE

Naomi Martinez was quite happy coming home from school on her bike. Naomi was a sixteen-year-old junior at Cesar Chavez High School. She had a nice boyfriend— Ernesto Sandoval. She was doing well in her classes. Now she was starting her first real job this afternoon at Chill Out, the yogurt shop.

Only a few months ago, Naomi was dating Clay Aguirre, a handsome junior with a bad temper. They'd been together a long time when his chronic rudeness turned to violence. One day he got mad at Naomi and punched her in the face. She'd cared for him for many years. Yet she found the courage to break up. Although Clay continued to hope to get back with her, it was completely over for Naomi. She was falling in love with Ernesto.

Naomi jumped off her bike and rolled it into the family garage. She didn't have to go to work for an hour. Naomi heard Brutus, the family pit bull, barking a loud greeting. Whenever family members came home, Brutus was thrilled to see them. When the Martinez family first got Brutus, Naomi's mother was terrified of the dog. Now Brutus had won her over too.

As Naomi was opening the front door, her father's pickup truck pulled into the driveway. The hairs on the back of Naomi's neck stood up. She could always tell when something was wrong with her father by the way he drove. He roared into the driveway now and slammed on the brakes. He was angry.

Naomi loved her father, but he was a hard man to deal with. Felix Martinez had already kicked his two older sons out of the house after bitter family fights. Orlando and Manuel had not spoken a word to their father now in years. The rift was deep and bitter.

Naomi's father considered himself the unquestioned ruler of the family. Everybody had to dance to his tune or else. Linda Martinez, Naomi's mother, was a timid woman who obeyed him completely. Years ago, when her husband hit her, she accepted even that abuse. She never dared to oppose Felix Martinez.

Naomi's father got out of the pickup. Right away, Naomi could see he had not come directly home. He worked as a heavy equipment operator, guiding a big crane. It was hard, dangerous work, and he was good at it. He'd started as a forklift operator but quickly learned the heavier equipment. On any day he had to work, he was very careful not to drink.

But it was Friday, the beginning of the weekend. Dad had stopped at his favorite bar and had a few drinks. Naomi hated that her father drank and then drove, even though it was only a few blocks. He was a good driver. He'd never had a DUI or an accident. But he still came out of that bar and got behind the wheel of the truck. Every time he did, he was putting his life and the lives of other people on the road with him at risk. And that was inexcusable.

"Hi Dad," Naomi greeted him. "How's everything?"

"How do you think it is, girl?" Dad barked. "My back aches. I had a lousy, miserable day with those idiots I gotta work with. Nobody knows what they're doing. I gotta stop my work and get them going right. I'm telling you, I'm working with morons. I'm trying to get the crane in position. They're jumping around like idiots in front of me. I don't know where they get those people."

"I'm sorry, Dad," Naomi sympathized. "Why don't you take a nice hot bath? That always makes you feel better."

"Nothin' makes me feel better anymore," Dad fumed. "I'm gettin' too old for this, girl. I'm almost fifty years old. I'm the old man down there now, except for Eppy and Pogo. You know how old fifty is? My old man was dead when he was fifty-five. Dropped dead of a heart attack. Worked himself to death. That's gonna be me in a coupla years, and who cares?"

Felix Martinez followed Naomi into the house. "Linda," he yelled at his wife. "It askin' too much for you to leave the soap you're watching on TV. Maybe you could drop that trashy celebrity magazine you got your nose in. How 'bout makin' me a cup of coffee? I need to sit down and have a cup of coffee. A man ought to be able to get that in his own house."

Dad looked at Naomi and declared, "Your mother don't do nothin' all day. All she does is read about those celebrities and watch trash soap operas."

Naomi bit her tongue. She never saw her mother reading a celebrity magazine. The only television she watched was the food network. She spent most of the day doing laundry, cleaning the house, and fixing meals. There wasn't a lazy bone in Mom's body.

"I'm getting the coffee, Felix!" Mom hollered from the kitchen. "Just sit down, and I'll bring it in."

Dad sank into his favorite leather chair in the living room. He closed his eyes and sighed, "Yeah, gonna be fifty next month. The end of next month. The big five-oh. I thought things would be different when I got this old. Fifty years on this stinking planet, and what have I got to show for it? A wife who won't do any more than she needs to. Two sons who don't care if I'm dead or alive. Scum of the earth. Lousy bums is what they are. I worked like a dog for my family. I spent a ton of money getting Orlando's teeth fixed at that crooked dentist's office. I did that just so the kid would look good. What thanks do I get for it? Orlando, he raised his hand against me, against his own father. He knocked me down. What kind of a son is that?"

Naomi dropped her backpack by the door and sat down on the sofa. She didn't know what to say. A few years ago, both Orlando and Manuel were thrown out of the house. Orlando had struck his father. Manuel had not obeyed the rules. Dad hadn't seen the boys since. But Ernesto Sandoval sneaked Naomi and her mother to secret meetings at small restaurants in town to visit with them. Naomi and her mother were very happy to see the boys. But they always feared that Dad would find out and fly into a rage. To him, the secret visits would be a betrayal of his authority.

Both Orlando and Manny were now doing well, working with the Oscar Perez Latin band. Orlando was a singer and gui-tarist, and Manny worked on the equip-ment. They worked mainly in Los Angeles, two hundred miles away. Naomi's dream was that someday her family could be healed. She hoped that Dad would accept the boys back and that they could all be friends again. But that dream seemed almost impossible, given Dad's bitterness. Dad often said he would forgive Orlando only if he apologized for hitting his father. Orlando swore he would never apologize. He'd struck his father to keep him from hitting Mom. So father and son were at a terrible impasse.

Linda Martinez brought the coffee in to her husband. "Here, Felix, this will make you feel much better," Mom said. She hopped nervously around Dad's chair like a little bird. She set the coffee on the end table where he could reach it.

Felix Martinez tasted the coffee. "It's too sweet," he complained, almost spitting out the mouthful. "Whadja do, woman? Pour the whole bag of sugar in here? You trying to kill me? You want to give me diabetes or something?"

"Felix, I put in three teaspoons of sugar like I always do," Linda Martinez explained. "You said you wanted three teaspoons of sugar."

"Get rid of this and get me some decent coffee," he commanded. He slammed the cup down on the table so hard that it splashed on the wood. Naomi's mother snatched it up, wiped up the spill, and scurried to the kitchen. Naomi got up and followed her mother.

"Mom," Naomi whispered, "he stopped at that bar on his way home from work. Two drinks makes him mellow. On the third drink he turns into a bear."

"It's the birthday coming up that's got to him," Mom groaned. "He feels old, Naomi. He feels like life has passed him by. And then his cousin, that Monte Esposito, getting voted out of office. That hit him hard. He was so proud of having his cousin on the city council. It made him feel like somebody. Now that's gone too, and Monte is in trouble with the law. And worst of all, the boys being estranged like they are. That eats at him. He likes to pretend he doesn't care, but he does. He loved those boys, still does. He misses them. He really, *really* misses them."

"I'll bring him this cup, Mom," Naomi offered. "You just finish getting dinner." Naomi reached around her mother's thin shoulders and gave her a hug. "Love you, Mom," she told her mother.

"Here Dad," Naomi said, putting the new cup of coffee down on the end table. "This isn't as sweet."

Felix Martinez started drinking the new coffee. "Yeah, this is better. I can't believe that woman has been married to me for almost thirty years. She still can't make coffee like I want it." Of course, Mom had put the same amount of sugar in the second cup.

"I'm starting my new job at Chill Out, the yogurt place," Naomi told her dad. "I'll be starting in about an hour. It's my first real job. I've had little jobs before. But this'll be the first one where I'm making some money."

Naomi's father turned and looked at his daughter. "I had my first job when I was fifteen. I was a soda jerk in this old drugstore. It was one of the last places that had soda fountains. I liked the job. I was a kid. When you're a kid, it's all new and exciting, and fun. You don't know what's gonna happen next. You got your whole life in front of you."

Felix Martinez sipped his coffee and stared at the wall. "When you're old like me, you know what's gonna happen next—nothin'. It's all behind you. The best days are behind you. Now you know they weren't all that hot anyway."

"You're not old, Dad," Naomi protested. "You're in the prime of your life."

Naomi's father laughed bitterly. "Yeah, right, like they say, fifty is the new thirty. What a crock. The new thirty with wrinkles and graying hair and bad feet and some other stuff I won't even talk about. You know the only thing gives me any satisfaction? It's my boy, Zack. Zack, he's loyal to me."

Dad turned to his daughter. "Naomi, you're my girl and I love you. But you ain't always loyal. You went behind my back. You stabbed the whole family in the back. You joined those *Zapatistas* who were backing that fool Ibarra for city council. You went against my wishes and against our blood. Monte Esposito is blood."

Felix Martinez seemed to be gathering steam. "Ibarra is a clown. That's what he is, nothing but a clown with a big mustache. Monte was doing a great job down there. Now it ain't bad enough they kicked him out for something he never done. Ibarra is behind that. Now they want to send my cousin to prison. That's the kind of people you threw in with, girl."

Naomi sat there silently. Anybody who kept up with city politics knew that Monte Esposito stopped serving the needs of the people in the *barrio* a long time ago. After a while, he was just helping himself and his cronies. Anybody who knew what was happening already saw Mr. Ibarra was getting the job done. He was putting in great new programs for the veterans and the young.

not at first, but you're smart. You'll get the hang of it. And, hey, you're a beautiful girl. Don't take nothin' from guys who're getting outta line, you hear me?"

"Yeah, thanks Dad," Naomi responded.

Naomi hurried to her room and changed her clothes. About ten minutes later, she heard Ernesto pull into the driveway. Usually he came in and said hello to whoever was there, but this time Naomi rushed out before he could get out of the car. She didn't want a confrontation between Ernesto and Dad.

Naomi ran up to the Volvo and said, "Hi Ernie. Let's just go. Dad is in kind of a bad mood."

Ernesto frowned. "Now what's the matter?" he asked.

"Oh," Naomi replied, as she got into the Volvo," he's obsessing about turning fifty. He's like thinking this is the end of the world or something. He's digging up all his old resentments and problems. He's saying he hasn't anything to show for his life and stuff."

"Zack's a good guy," Naomi concurred. She loved Zack, but she loved her missing brothers too.

"You bet he is," Dad agreed. "Zack— he's there for me and the family one hundred percent. He never joined those lousy *Zapatistas*. He was going around trying to help Monte Esposito. That's what he was doing. Trying to convince those fools out there that they had pure gold in Monte. But most people are too stupid to see the truth even if it hits them in the face."

Zack was seventeen, going on eighteen. He was done with high school. Now he was taking classes at the community college. He was pretty aimless, but he did whatever his father asked. He never even came close to defying Felix Martinez, as Naomi had done.

"Well, I guess it's time for me to go to work," Naomi announced. "I don't want to be late on my first day. Ernesto will be picking me up to take me over there. It's real close to Chavez High. So maybe I can work it out with somebody else on my shift to come home with them."

"I don't think that much of that Ernesto Sandoval either," Mr. Martinez commented. He ignored what Naomi had to say. "He was one of those *Zapatistas*. He talks a good game, but he's a snake in the grass."

Naomi started toward the hallway but stopped when her father had more to say. "I think he's the one turned you around, Naomi. You always been a good loyal family girl, but he undermined you there."

Naomi stood at the head of the hallway. She desperately wanted to get away from her father—to get to her room. "I think you'd of been better off sticking with Clay Aguirre," her Dad went on. "He worked hard for Monte Esposito. Clay's got his faults, but he was true blue when it came to that election. He and Zack were working side by side, passing out flyers. Clay is a real guy. Sandoval is one of those wimps who can go either way. You can't trust 'em. Ernie is like his father, one of these

phonies who want to take money from hard-working stiffs like me and hand it over to the bums who won't work."

Naomi wanted to say, "Daddy, Clay Aguirre punched me in the face. Clay Aguirre punched *your daughter* in the face. I was all black and blue. My cheek was swollen, and I couldn't see out of one eye. Even before then, he was rude an insulting. Why didn't you care about m Daddy? Why weren't you enraged tha boy like Clay Aguirre would punch y daughter in the face?"

But saying that would just get Da riled up. Naomi didn't want any trouble, for herself or for Mom. Sh wanted to get out of there and go tc "Well, I'm going to change my cloth I'll be home around ten," she state

Mr. Martinez looked up, his ey ing on his daughter. The effec drinks at the bar were wearin coffee had helped too. "Well, there on the job, girl. It ain't go

She buckled up, and Ernesto backed the car out of the driveway. "Dad figures," Naomi went on, "that he's gonna die pretty soon even though he's in good health. I mean, he's really morose. I think not being in touch with Orlando and Manny is a big deal to him. He acts like he doesn't care, like it's 'good riddance to bad rubbish.' But that's not how he feels in his heart."

Ernesto just listened, as Naomi went on. "They were his first two sons, Orlando and Manny. You should see the photos in the albums, of those boys and Dad. You know, him holding them on his shoulders, the three of them laughing and cutting up. He looks so proud and happy, Ernie. It's enough to break your heart that he hasn't seen them in years. He puts on that bold front, but I think it's eating him alive."

"There's gotta be a way to bring the family together again," Ernesto declared.

"Oh Ernie, I think about it all the time," Naomi lamented. "Dad has always said he won't forgive Orlando for hitting him

17

unless my brother apologizes. Orlando says he won't apologize because he was defending Mom. Orlando is thickheaded and stubborn, just like Dad. He won't bend. And Manny goes along with Orlando. He wouldn't make up with Dad if Orlando isn't part of the deal. Manny is really close with Orlando."

"But still," Ernesto objected, "there's gotta be a way to resolve it." They were nearing the Chill Out yogurt shop, where Naomi now worked. Ernesto turned to Naomi and asked, "Are you nervous about starting work?"

"A little bit," Naomi admitted. "The boss is a guy about fifty, I guess. And his son does the managing. They seem nice."

"Naomi, when I started work at the pizzeria I was really nervous," Ernesto confessed. "But you'll be fine." He continued looking at Naomi and said, "You're so beautiful. The customers . . . the guys . . . they're gonna be flirting with you, girl. I bet some of them'll hit on you."

"Oh, we wear these dumb aprons and caps with the snowman logo. That's not exactly high fashion," Naomi said, laughing.

"Babe, you could be wearing a tarp, and you'd still knock 'em dead," Ernesto told her.

Naomi got out of the Volvo and Ernesto suggested, "Let me pick you up after work tonight. Then, if you want to work something out with another employee to take you home, okay. But the first time I'd like to come pick you up."

"Sure, Ernie, thanks," Naomi agreed, leaning over and kissing him.

When Naomi got into Chill Out, Sherry Carranza, the crew leader, greeted her. "You're early, Naomi. I like that. Gives me a chance to show you around. Jimmy'll be here in about thirty minutes."

Jimmy Ancho, the boss's son, had hired Naomi. She had yet to meet the boss, Elia Ancho. Sherry said he came around a lot to keep his eyes on the business. Another yogurt shop in this location had failed. Now

Chill Out was striving not to make the same mistakes that drove the first store out of business.

Sherry was in her midtwenties, pretty but not beautiful. She seemed very smart. She showed Naomi where the toppings were kept. There were chocolate and butterscotch chips, several kinds of nuts, raisins, even fruit. All of it was served on top of the yogurt. "The toppings are what keeps a place like this profitable," Sherry explained. "People coming in for plain chocolate or vanilla frozen yogurt. You don't make much money. So we don't ask a customer, 'Do you want a topping?' Instead, we say, 'What kind of a topping would you like for your yogurt?' That makes all the difference."

Naomi had told all her friends at Chavez High that she was starting here tonight. Many of them promised to come in. Familiar faces began to appear around eight o'clock. Carmen Ibarra came in with her new boyfriend, Paul Morales. Abel Ruiz came in with his girl, Claudia Villa. They all ordered frozen yogurts—loaded with toppings.

Then, to Naomi's annoyance, Clay Aguirre came in with Mira Nuñez. "Hey Naomi," Clay hollered. "You look kinda tired. Doesn't she look tired, Mira? You lost some weight, girl? You got problems? Doesn't she look sort of gaunt, Mira?"

Mira just shrugged and ordered her yogurt. It irked her to no end that Clay continued to be obsessed with Naomi. Mira had tried everything to be attractive to Clay. Yet he kept thinking about Naomi Martinez.

When Mira excused herself to go to the restroom, Clay Aguirre drew closer to Naomi. "Hey babe," he told her, "why do you keep fighting it? You miss me. You miss what we had together. You want it just like it was in the old days. Ernie Sandoval is a poor substitute for the real deal, Naomi. You just say the word. It'll be the same as it used to be, you and me against the world. Mira, she don't mean anything to me."

"What kind of topping do you want?" Naomi asked in a cold voice.

"Something sweet, like you, babe," Clay replied. He leaned his elbows on the counter and got into Naomi's face.

Naomi added some chocolate chips to Clay's yogurt and took his money. She never once met his eyes. When Naomi turned a moment later, she noticed that the boss, Elia Ancho, had come in. He was a handsome man with silver hair. He had apparently been watching Naomi's encounter with Clay Aguirre. Now he walked over to where Naomi was working. He commented, "You handled the masher real well, young lady."

"Thank you," Naomi said. "Thank you, Mr. Ancho." Elia Ancho headed for the kitchen, where his son was. Naomi heard him say, "That new girl—she's stunning. Absolutely stunning."

CHAPTER TWO

The rest of the evening went well. Other friends from Chavez came in. Naomi made a few mistakes, but she learned fast. Sherry told her she was a very quick employee. Naomi was so happy with the way everything was going that she forgot all about the scene with Clay.

At quarter to nine, Ernesto pulled up in the parking lot next to Chill Out. He never noticed the Mustang in the darkness. Nor did he see the young man leaning against the door. "Hey Sandoval," Clay yelled, "still driving your granny's car, huh? It fits you."

Ernesto ignored Clay. But Clay was not to be denied. "I got news for you, dude.

I was in there getting frozen yogurt, and Naomi was really sweet to me. She looked at me with those gorgeous violet eyes and she smiled. Boy, did she smile. I think it's all coming back to her, the times we had. I think you're gonna have a problem keeping the girl interested in you, man. Sorry, but that's how it's going down."

"You're blowing smoke, Aguirre," Ernesto responded. "Naomi is so done with you."

"You think?" Clay taunted. "Then how come she said maybe she and I could hang together sometime. You know, just for old times' sake. I'm telling you, man, the chick is getting tired of you. She had the best. She's not going to settle for second best now."

"She wants you back as much as she wants last year's flu man," Ernesto said.

"Sandoval, you're scared," Clay badgered Ernesto. "I can see it in your eyes. You're wondering if maybe what I'm saying has a little truth in it. You're shaking inside, man. You're sweating. You're not all that sure of her."

Ernesto was wondering about Clay's crack about Naomi. Did Naomi really say she'd hang with him again? He couldn't believe it, but Clay had him going.

"Me and her," Clay persisted, "we had a lotta years together. You just been with her a few months. When we had that fight, you got her on the rebound man. But that's all over now. She knows she acted too fast. She's having regrets. I apologized to her. Now she's sorry she didn't accept that. She wants to be back with the guy she really has the hots for. A girl needs some excitement in her life, Sandoval. You're about as exciting as cold oatmeal."

The door of the Chill Out opened, and Naomi came out. The first thing she saw was Clay Aguirre leaning on his Mustang and yelling at Ernesto.

"Are you still here, Clay?" Naomi snapped. "Have you been hanging around here all that time? What's *wrong* with you?

I've told you before, Clay. If you don't stop harassing me, I'm going to tell the cops that you're stalking me. I don't want to do that, but I will."

Ernesto felt a lot better than he had a moment ago. "Get lost, man," Ernesto told Clay.

Clay Aguirre said nothing. He got in his Mustang and drove away. Naomi got in with Ernesto, and he asked, "How was day one, babe?"

"It was wonderful, Ernie," Naomi bubbled. "The customers were all nice and friendly. Sherry, the team boss, she says I'm learning faster than anybody she's seen. The owners, Mr. Ancho and his son, were so nice. I love the job. The only bad thing that happened was Clay coming in when I was just starting to work. He was making all these stupid comments."

"He said you were real anxious to get back with him," Ernesto remarked, laughing.

Naomi shook her head in disbelief. "I'm telling you, Ernie," she said, "Clay is starting to act *sick*. I've seen him outside my house late at night, just sitting there. He really, *really* gives me the creeps. I think I'll call his parents and ask them to take him to a therapist or something."

"I'm sorry, babe," Ernesto sympathized. "I'm sorry he messed up your big night."

"Yeah," Naomi replied. She shrugged, as if trying to lift a weight from her shoulders. "Now I'm going home, and I'm hoping and praying Dad has gone to bed early. I'm in no mood to hear what a terrible life he's had and why his boys are so evil."

Ernesto dropped Naomi off at her place. He waited in the driveway, the car motor running for a few seconds. Then Naomi appeared in the doorway, giving him a thumbs-up. Ernesto smiled and drove home.

When Naomi came into the Martinez household, Zack was playing video games. He looked up and asked, "How was your job, Sis?"

"It was good," Naomi replied. "I got the hang of everything real fast. They seem to like me."

Naomi sat down on the sofa, tired, and looked at Zack. He was a nice-looking kid, but not as handsome as Orlando. Who could be as handsome as Orlando? But Zack was cuter than Manny. But they were all nice-looking guys. "How's college, Zack?" she asked.

"Ah, kinda boring," he responded, still working on his video game. "It's like high school never stopped. I'd like to quit right now and go into the construction business like Dad. I've watched Dad operating that heavy machinery, and it really gets me excited. I'd love to do stuff like that. I think it's cool how he works that huge crane."

"Have you noticed, Zack," Naomi inquired, "that Dad is kinda down lately? He feels bad about turning fifty and stuff. He's sort of depressed."

Zack shrugged. While Naomi was talking, he'd finished his video game and was texting a friend. He did that constantly, even at the dinner table. He didn't pay much attention to what people were saying to him.

"Zack, do you miss Orlando and Manny?" Naomi asked.

"I don't know," Zack replied. "I guess so. It seems weird that they never come around, but they really messed up. Dad says they're bums, and I guess that's right. I think Orlando is doing music with that Oscar Perez band or something. I never seen him. I don't believe he really sings and plays the guitar. He probably just carries stuff around or drives the bus. Dad says my brothers are gonna end up like those bums in the ravine. I guess they got it coming 'cause they didn't respect Dad. A kid should respect his father."

"I think deep down Dad misses Orlando and Manny," Naomi said. "He has too much pride to say so. But I think one of the reasons he feels so sad is that he hasn't seen his sons in years. I was thinking, wouldn't it be great if we could arrange for a way for our brothers to come to a fiftieth birthday party for Dad? I think that would be the best gift Dad could get."

Zack had started texting again, but now he stopped abruptly. He looked at Naomi with alarm. "Dad wouldn't let them in the house, Naomi," he protested. "He hates them. He told me that. He said if they showed up around here, he'd call the police. Orlando did a really bad thing. He hit Dad, and Dad fell on the floor. Dad could never forgive Orlando for that."

"Zack," Naomi asked, "do you know why Orlando was so angry with Dad that he did that?"

Zack was silent for a few seconds. He looked very confused and unhappy. "I wasn't here when it happened," he finally replied. "When I got home, Dad had thrown all of Orlando's stuff out of the house. But, you know, right after it happened, Orlando called me. He tried to turn me against Dad. Orlando, he told me a bunch of lies. He said Dad was hurting Mom, and that's why he hit him. Dad loves Mom. Dad would never hurt her. I think if the house was on fire, Dad would go right through the flames to save Mom."

Zack continued texting but kept talking too. "Maybe . . . you know, Dad was mad and he pushed Mom a little or something. But he didn't mean anything. It was wrong for Orlando to hit Dad. I told Orlando not to call me anymore, and he didn't."

Naomi decided not to say anymore. Felix Martinez had just one son left, and Naomi couldn't understand his relationship with Dad. Zack was the only member of the family who gave him real satisfaction. Naomi was not about to take that away from her father. She knew what Orlando said was true. Dad was slapping Mom, and Orlando couldn't take it. But Naomi couldn't tell Zack the truth. Naomi loved and pitied her father, even though she knew he had done a bad thing. Zack was the only son left who respected his father unconditionally.

Naomi went into the kitchen, where her mother was taking a batch of cookies from the oven. "Mmm, those smell good, Mom," she remarked.

"Take one, sweetheart," Linda Martinez urged her. "You're so skinny, you don't have to worry about eating sweets. I baked them for my little social tomorrow. I'm really looking forward to that. Wednesdays are the highlight of my week."

Every Wednesday, Linda Martinez got together with lady friends, mostly from Our Lady of Guadalupe Church. Maria Sandoval, Liza Ruiz, and several other women were in the group. They met at each other's houses, but the Martinez house was never in the rotation. Felix Martinez thought the women were a bunch of lazy gossips. He didn't want them around even when he was at work. Naomi had the feeling that her father resented his wife having any social life that didn't involve her family.

"Mom, I keep thinking and thinking," Naomi commented. "Wouldn't it be wonderful if we could find a way to get our family back together again? Dad was saying how terrible it is that his two older sons are gone. I know it hurts him, all that bitterness. For his fiftieth birthday, maybe we could work something out for a reconciliation."

Mom looked almost frightened. "Oh Naomi," Mrs. Martinez fretted, "he would never stand for them coming back. Never. Don't even mention such a thing to him. He would fly into a terrible rage. He would be even angrier than he already is."

Naomi looked at her mother and felt terribly sad. That was how her mother lived her life—in fear. Don't rock the boat, even if it is sinking in a sea of sharks. Whatever you do, endure your familiar, miserable life. The alternative could be even worse.

Naomi wondered whether her mother was always like this. Or did she get this way after living all these years with Felix Martinez? When Mom was a young girl, didn't she have any courage even then? Did she always choose going with the flow, even though the river was heading for the rapids? Did she never realize that not taking a risk was maybe the most dangerous choice of all? Did she ever think that being passive shut off any dreams of a better future?

Naomi went to her room and called Orlando on her cell phone. "Hey Orlando, how's it going?" she asked.

"We're getting more gigs all the time, Naomi," Orlando responded. "So how was your first night at the yogurt shop?"

Naomi and Mom had gotten together for secret dinners with Orlando and Manny behind Dad's back. Ernesto had driven Naomi and her mother to little out-of-the-way restaurants, where they hugged and kissed and talked. The get-togethers meant the world to Mom, as long as her husband never found out. Now Naomi regularly called her brothers and shared her life with them.

"Everything went good, Orlando," Naomi responded. "I love the job, and they seem to like me."

But Naomi hadn't called her brother to chitchat. She started asking the question she wanted to ask. "Uh . . . Orlando . . . with his fiftieth birthday coming up, Dad is so depressed."

"Yeah?" Orlando responded, not sure where Naomi was going.

"You know," Naomi went on, "next month he's going to be fifty. He thinks that's really old and the best times are all behind him. And, Orlando, he feels really bad that he never sees you guys, you and Manny."

"He say that?" Orlando asked in a skeptical voice. "What did he *really* say?"

"Just that," Naomi said carefully. "You know, all he did for you guys when you were growing up and now you're just . . . you know . . . *gone*."

"Come on, Sis," Orlando insisted, "you're editing it. He called us rotten names, didn't he? I know the old *diablo*. He's not sitting around being sentimental that his two boys don't come to visit him no more. He's saying what monsters we are, right?" Orlando's voice was angry.

"Yeah, that's right, Orlando," Naomi admitted. "But Orlando, I know him. It hurts him deeply, even though he won't admit it. I can see the pain in his eyes."

"Naomi, you're a sweet kid," Orlando told his sister. "You got a big heart. I love you for that, but you're seeing something that just isn't there. The old *diablo* has turned against me and Manny, and that ain't ever gonna change. You're looking at the situation through rose-colored glasses, Sis."

Naomi knew Orlando was right. She couldn't object. "Remember Uncle Leon," Orlando went on, "Dad's brother? Remember how he turned against his poor daughter just because she married a dude he didn't like? Remember how he refused to forgive her even when he lay dying? That's Dad too. Guys like that, they don't have real hearts. Their hearts are made of stone."

Naomi remembered being fourteen, at the hospital when Uncle Leon was dying.

His daughter, her cousin, was in the hall screaming, "Daddy! Daddy! Daddy!" But she never received her father's forgiveness.

"Orlando," Naomi said in a suddenly fierce voice, "it's not going to be that way with our family! I love you guys, you and Manny, and I love him too. He's not an old *diablo*, Orlando. He's our father. He's messed up, I know. But it's not going to be like it was with Uncle Leon. I'm going to think of something to bring us together. Orlando, will you promise me that if I think of something, you'll work with me? You won't be hard-hearted and refuse to work with me, will you?"

"Listen girl I'd do anything for you," Orlando said, with more softness in his voice. "You know that. I'll play the game even though I know it's going nowhere. I'll show up at the house carrying a birthday cake for the old *diab*- . . . for our father. I'll dress like a clown and dance on the lawn. I'll bring my guitar and sing him a song. But if he gets a shotgun and comes after me, I'll run as fast as I can. You just gotta help me get away before he starts shooting, okay?"

Naomi smiled. "Okay Orlando. Maybe I won't even come up with anything. But I'm going to try. I don't want to be in some hospital corridor someday. I don't want Daddy dying with you and Manny unforgiven."

"Keep me posted, *mi hermana*," Orlando said. "How's Ernie?"

"He's wonderful as usual," Naomi replied.

"You got a good one there, girl," Orlando advised. "The Oscar Perez band'll be coming down there pretty soon, and we gotta get together. You and Mom and us. How is Mama?"

"Oh, she's okay," Naomi responded. "Tomorrow she has her Wednesday social. She and her friends go to each other's houses and just visit. That means a lot to Mom."

"But they never come to our house, do they?" Orlando asked.

"Well, no," Naomi admitted.

"The old *diablo* wouldn't allow that," Orlando commented bitterly. "He doesn't like to see Mom having a little fun."

"Orlando, please don't call him that," Naomi pleaded. "He's my father. He's *our* father. He works hard, and he's kept the family going. He's not one hundred percent bad."

"Ninety-nine percent?" Orlando teased.

"Orlando! Stop it!" Naomi demanded.

"I'm sorry, *mi hermana*," Orlando apologized. "I'll try to repent. Really I will."

They said their good-byes, and Naomi slid the phone shut. She had no idea what she might do to end the rift in her family. But she had to do something. She just couldn't let it go on and on until it was too late. From time to time, Naomi and her mother saw Uncle Leon's daughter, the one he couldn't forgive. She was now married, and she had a nice family of her own. She seemed happy. But there was always a sadness in her eyes. It was the remnant of unfinished business, a breach never healed.

In the morning at the Martinez house, Naomi could hear the local news on the television. That was unusual. She came from her bedroom in her pajamas and robe. Usually her parents watched television only in the evening or on an afternoon when football was on. Now the TV was blaring loudly.

Naomi saw her father sitting at the edge of his chair, a steady stream of curses escaping his lips.

"They indicted Monte," he cried in anguish. "They indicted the guy. It ain't bad enough he lost his job on the city council to that clown, Ibarra. Now those jackals are coming after him to try to put him in jail. They want to put Monte in jail when he never done nothin' but help people. The guy has a heart of gold. And listen to those jackals going on there."

Naomi listened to the television anchor-woman. She was talking about the bar and grill owned by the Saenz brothers. For a long time, they had wanted to open up their place. But the local people protested that the *barrio* already had too many places to buy liquor. The neighbors fought tooth and nail. They put together petitions and went before the city council. For a while, it seemed they would be able to stop the bar and grill from opening. Then the vote was held, and it came down to a tie. Monte Esposito broke the tie by voting for the Saenz brothers. Then it was full speed ahead. Now the grand jury had indicted Monte Esposito. The charge was that he had received a bribe to influence his vote.

"Listen to those jackals," Dad raved on. "Monte never took no bribe. What are they talking about? There ain't a more honest man in the whole *barrio*."

Mom had come from the kitchen. She softly asked, "Do you want some coffee, Felix?"

"Are you nuts?" he ranted. "Do I look like I want to drink coffee with all this

41

going on?" He seemed close to tears. "My cousin, my best buddy . . . look at what they're doing to him? I can't believe this."

Monte Esposito had gotten Dad tickets to football games and invitations to ritzy parties. He was Felix Martinez's link to a world he never would have seen without Monte. Dad even got his picture taken with the president of the United States. The president had come to speak on behalf of a congressional candidate. Monte got into that party, and he made sure his cousin Felix got there too. That was the kind of relationship they had.

"Don't get so upset, Felix," Mom cautioned. "You have high blood pressure anyway."

"I don't care about that," Felix Martinez cried. "It's a lynch mob right there. They're tryin' to lynch Monte. They'll probably arrest him and book him in a day or so."

The television anchorwoman commented soberly. "This may be the worst case of political corruption in the city's history." Dad slammed his fist on the arm of his chair and cursed loudly.

"Listen to this!" Felix Martinez screamed. "Now this idiot anchorwoman is saying they got another investigation going. It's about that old bum who fell in the wash just before the election. They're trying to connect poor Monte with his death. Why don't they just bring a rope and hang Monte on a tree?"

"Felix," Mom sang, "breakfast is ready. You need to come and eat. That'll make you feel better."

"I'm supposed to eat the slop you made?" he snarled. "And that's gonna make me feel okay about them lynchin' my cousin? Is that what you're sayin'? You're even dumber than I thought."

Felix Martinez was storming. "This guy, Monte, we been like brothers for most of my life. I care about this guy. He come through for me a ton of times. He never forgot me when he got to be a big shot. He coulda been down there at city hall acting like he was too good for his relatives and friends. But not Monte. He stayed the same good guy he used to be when us kids were playing stickball in the streets. Monte don't deserve what's happenin' to him."

The man whom Mr. Martinez called a "bum" was a homeless war veteran. His name was Rezzi. Actually, his real name was David Juarez, but everyone knew him as Rezzi. The man used to work for Monte Esposito. When Rezzi was fired, he took some papers from Esposito's office. The documents showed that the councilman was a criminal.

Just before the election, Rezzi decided to turn the evidence over to the district attorney. He told his friend, Julio Avila's father, that he was going to do it. But he also left word at the councilman's office that he was going to the DA. That night, Rezzi drowned in a wash near the ravine where he lived.

Did Monte Esposito or his friends kill Rezzi to keep him quiet? If so, killing Rezzi hadn't worked. Mr. Avila got the documents and turned them over to the authorities.

The idea that the councilman might have had Rezzi killed made Naomi very nervous. She suspected that Monte Esposito had been pulling fast ones for a long time. But she also thought he'd covered his tracks well enough to avoid getting caught. Naomi never liked Monte Esposito. She thought he was a loudmouth and probably a crook. But even now she couldn't believe he could be a murderer.

CHAPTER THREE

Naomi was glad to get out of the house and head for school. Dad would be going to work soon, and that was good. With him out of the house, Mom could go visit with the other ladies. Maybe, Naomi thought, by tonight Dad would be cooled off. Still, today wasn't the end of the Monte Esposito story. No doubt the excouncilman had good lawyers. They'd probably engineer some plea bargain on the bribery charges. But if he was connected to the death of Rezzi, that was a whole other thing. Naomi didn't want to think about Dad's reaction.

When Naomi saw Ernesto at school, she rushed up to him and asked, "Ernie did you hear?"

"Yeah, Esposito and the Saenz brothers got indicted," Ernesto replied. "Everybody was really steamed when the bar and grill got passed when nobody wanted it. My dad says, if you want to see a neighborhood going down the drain, just look for a bar on every block. They suck the life right out of an area."

"My dad is just furious about Monte's troubles," Naomi remarked, shuddering. "He was like a madman this morning, saying they're trying to lynch Esposito. You know, he was feeling bad enough about turning fifty next month. Now this. All his frustration and demons are closing in on him. I'm telling you, Ernie, my house is not a happy place right now."

Ernesto put his arm around Naomi's shoulders. "I'm sorry, babe," he consoled her. "I know it can't be easy. I bet your poor Mom is catching it too."

"Yeah," Naomi admitted, "but she and some other ladies are going over to your house today. Those weekly Wednesday get-togethers keep Mom sane, I think. Last night Mom baked some wonderful little macaroons for her gang."

"Yeah," Ernesto said. "Mom told me she was having the girls over today. It means a lot to my mom too. I think it's great. You know, women talk more than men about personal stuff. The ladies need to get together like they do. Mom told me this morning she's making a lot of coffee. You know, since my mom got her children's book published, she's been talking at some bookstores. And she likes that. But her mother, my grandma, she calls like every other day asking Mom when she's writing another book. She's asking how much will they pay her and stuff like that. It's kinda hard."

But Naomi's mind was on other things. "Ernie," she asked, "did you hear that they're looking into Rezzi's death now too?"

"Yeah," Ernesto acknowledged. "The night before he was going to the DA with his evidence against Monte Esposito, he drowns in the wash. That sort of looks bad."

"Ernie," Naomi said in an anxious voice, "Monte Esposito is family. Ever since I was a little girl, he's had dinner with us at least once a month. I never liked him. He's one of those loud, backslapping kind of guys. But I can't believe he would ever be involved in a murder. I mean, that's so horrifying."

"Well, maybe he's not," Ernesto suggested. "Of course, maybe Esposito or his friends knew Rezzi was going to the DA. Maybe they figured their lives were about to go up in smoke. I don't know. People do desperate things when their backs are to the wall."

"I still just won't believe it," Naomi objected. "Not murder."

At lunchtime, Naomi saw Julio Avila buying a grape soda at the vending machine. Naomi walked over and asked, "Julio, you heard that they're looking into Rezzi's death."

A big smile came to Julio's face. "Yeah," he beamed, "the whole stinking mess is comin' apart. My dad is really happy about that. Pop said Rezzi was a good, sweet guy. He worked for Esposito for a long time. Then he refused to do Esposito's dirty work. So he lost his job, and his whole life went down the drain. That was all Esposito's fault. Somebody has to pay for that, Naomi."

"But do you really think Monte Esposito had something to do with Rezzi drowning in that wash?" Naomi asked.

"Yeah, I do," Julio asserted. "Makes sense. Esposito had a lot to lose if Rezzi got those documents down to the DA. Only old Esposito didn't figure on Rezzi's pal, my pop. He found the envelope and got it to where it would do some good. The whole bribery indictment against Esposito comes from stuff in that envelope. Yeah, what goes around comes around. Now it's Monte's turn to slowly swing in the wind." Julio laughed.

"Monte Esposito is my father's cousin," Naomi remarked sadly. "My dad and him are really close. It's hit my dad hard."

"Oh, that's too bad, Naomi," Julio said. "But we all got rotten apples in the family tree, even closer than cousins. My old man, I love him. But he's done a lot of stuff I don't even want to know about. He's been a bum and a loser for a long time. He hung around down in the ravine and got to be friends with those other losers. They drank. They gambled. They got in fights."

Julio shook his head, as if he couldn't understand his dad. "Couple years ago," he went on, "two of the guys got in a fight over a bottle of whiskey. It was like a quarter full. The loser in that argument ended up dead. My pop saw the whole thing go down. 'Man,' I asked him, 'a guy died over a quarter of a bottle of whiskey? That was worth a man's life?' And Pop goes, 'If it's all they got in the world, it is.' "

Usually Naomi had lunch with Tessie Zamora, Carmen Ibarra, and Yvette Ozono.

But today she joined Ernesto and Abel Ruiz. Ernesto's father, Luis Sandoval, and Abel's father were nowhere near fifty. Naomi told the boys how bad her father felt about turning fifty.

Abel shrugged. "My dad is sort of like a patient mule. He gave up on being really happy a long time ago. Now he just looks for a little joy in small things. A good meal. A funny show on TV. He knows it's going downhill for him. So the birthdays don't mean much. Mom's different. When she turned forty, she freaked out. She started tracking down every gray hair in her head. Then she got a dye job. She even went and got some Botox. She really did. It's like she doesn't want to say good-bye to youth."

Naomi lay back on the grass and ate the peach she bought at the vending machine. "I wonder if we'll be like that when we're older," she mused. "Time seems to go slow now. I've heard it goes slow when you're young. Then, when you're older, it just races by. Sometimes I think I'll be in high school forever."

Ernesto laughed. "Babe," he chuckled, "I think it has to do with following your dreams. Just follow your dreams and give life a good shot. Then I don't think growing older is as bad. I want to do something that makes me really happy. That way, when I'm an old codger, I can remember the good things."

"Me too," Abel agreed. "I'm going to become the best chef in the country."

"My dad never talked about having dreams," Naomi commented. "I think when he was a kid, he just needed work. He got into construction, and that was it. He married Mom when he was twenty. I guess they were in love. Maybe they still are in their own way."

Julio Avila joined them then. "Track meet next week against Hillsdale, Ernie. You ready for it?" he asked.

"Yeah, I'm practicing a lot," Ernesto replied.

"My dad's real excited," Julio said. "He even got this little cheapie camera now so he can take pictures. He expects me to win all the races. I'm telling you, that's the only thing he gets a kick out of anymore. Just me running and winning. And, of course, he's happy they're going to bust Esposito for what he did to Rezzi."

"We don't know yet that Esposito is guilty," Naomi objected. Naomi thought that, if Monte was indicted for murder, it would be last straw for her father. His moods were getting angrier and darker lately. It was hard to imagine how he would take the news. He already thought the world was against him, even his two older sons. Felix Martinez thought his wife didn't care enough to please him. And he told Naomi she had not been loyal when she supported Emilio Ibarra for city council. Now, if his beloved cousin went down for murder . . .

"The cops are questioning all the guys in the ravine," Julio commented.

"Somebody had to have seen something. Maybe like somebody down there that night who didn't belong there. Maybe some thug working for Esposito. Or maybe they just paid some dude already down there to give Rezzi a push. Lot of those guys would do anything for a few bucks. Poor old Rezzi was weak and sickly. Wouldn't have taken much to just give him a shove."

Naomi was feeling sick. She closed her eyes. David Juarez had bravely served his country. He was once on the staff of a city councilman. And he came to his end in a muddy wash, perhaps a victim of a crime. The thought sickened her.

Naomi walked slowly to her next class after lunch, feeling depressed. She hated to think of going home and listening to her father's ranting. As she walked, she heard a familiar, if unwelcome voice.

"Hey Naomi," Clay Aguirre called.

"Clay, I thought you were going to stop bothering me," Naomi responded.

"I got something important to say, Naomi. You'll want to hear this," Clay said. He seemed serious.

"What is it?" Naomi sighed.

"I think I know something about what happened to that bum they called Rezzi," Clay confided.

"What are you talking about, Clay?" Naomi demanded. "How would you know anything about that?"

"They were saying on TV that your dad's cousin, Monte Esposito, is being investigated for that, you know," Clay explained. "I bet your dad's really worried. I think I found something out that'll help Monte Esposito. I think maybe I can put him in the clear. So I'd like to come over to your house and talk to your dad."

"Clay," Naomi groaned, "is this another of your tricks to get us back together again? I am so tired of this, Clay. Can't you just leave me alone?"

"No, no Naomi," Clay protested. "This is for real. I got a lot of respect for your father. If I can help his cousin out here, I'd like to do it."

Naomi stared at Clay Aguirre. She knew her father liked him. Clay's campaigning for Esposito really made a big impression on Naomi's father. But Naomi was deeply suspicious of what Clay was trying to do now. "Clay, come on. What's this really all about?" she demanded. "How could you have information about Rezzi's death?"

Clay's eyes narrowed. "I think I know who pushed Rezzi off the edge of that ravine, Naomi. I found out who sent him into those muddy waters, girl. I know exactly who did it. It had nothing to do with Monte Esposito or any of his friends. I was thinking about poor Monte getting blamed for it. So I went down into the ravine, and I started talking to some of the losers down there. I brought them sandwiches and some sodas. And, yeah, I gave them a few dollars to tell me what they know. I hit pay dirt right away, Naomi."

"You paid some of those poor bums to tell you fish stories for money, Clay," Naomi objected. "Some of those guys are so desperate they'd say anything for a sandwich. They gave you what you wanted to hear, whatever that was."

"No, I got the truth, Naomi," Clay insisted. "This one dude, he said there's a guy comes down most every day and gets friendly with the losers down there. He don't live in the ravine, but he wins their confidence. This guy got real close to Rezzi, got Rezzi to pour out his heart to him. Rezzi told this dude if anything ever happens to him, he needs to go to this tarp where Rezzi slept . . . collect pictures and letters and anything else that looks important. Rezzi had a wife and kids he hadn't heard from in a long time. He relied on this con man to send the personal effects on to his family if he kicked the bucket."

Naomi turned cold. She recognized who Clay Aguirre was talking about—Julio Avila's father. But he wasn't a con man. He was genuinely a friend to the men in the ravine, especially the veterans. Naomi stared at Clay, fearing the worst. Clay was trying to do something to please Naomi's father by clearing his cousin. But he was throwing Mr. Avila under the bus.

"Where's all this going, Clay?" Naomi asked. "I'm not believing any of it."

"One of the old dudes told me Rezzi had more than old pictures and letters," Clay explained. His eyes were burning with excitement. "He had money too. A coupla thousand. He was saving it for his family when he found them. Rezzi'd told this con man about the money. Well, that night the con man got tired of waiting for Rezzi to die. He started choking him. He demanded to know where the money was hidden. Then, when Rezzi told him, he pushed the old guy over the edge into the muddy wash. I know you don't want to hear this, Naomi. This con man—he's old man Avila. You and that jerk Sandoval are friends of his son, Julio."

"That's insane, Clay," Naomi protested. "Mr. Avila felt like a brother to Rezzi. He never would have harmed him. You're making this all up, Clay, and I don't want to listen to any more of your lies. Just go away and leave me alone."

"Your father's right, Naomi," Clay responded, shaking his head. "You got hard and mean because you're hanging with Sandoval. He's turned you around so you're not the same person anymore. You used to be a nice sweet chick. It's sad what you've turned into, girl."

Clay jerked his thumb over shoulder, as if pointing to someone behind him. "But these guys, they told me the truth. Wasn't it strange that right after Rezzi died, Avila had all his stuff? He had the pictures and the letters. He had that envelope that was full of lies about poor Monte Esposito. Avila wanted Monte to be blamed for Rezzi's death. Then nobody would be poking around to find the true murderer—old Avila himself. Whether you like it or not, I'm making sure everybody knows the truth, girl."

Naomi's head was spinning. She was sure Clay had gone down into the ravine to dig up a story. He probably paid those desperate men—drunks and drug addicts— to tell him some story that would clear Monte Esposito. And they pointed their fingers at Mr. Avila. Clay was just trying something else to get close to Naomi through her father. He knew Felix Martinez would be grateful if Clay got his cousin off the hook for Rezzi's death. Then maybe her father would pressure Naomi into forgiving Clay.

Yet, Naomi thought, maybe the story *was* true. Naomi remembered Mr. Avila's story about the two men fighting over a nearly empty whiskey bottle. One of the men was killed for it. Mr. Avila had told his son that a man might kill if that bottle of whiskey was all he had.

Naomi didn't know Mr. Avila. She only knew his son, and she didn't even know

Julio that well. Now she wondered, could Julio's father have pushed Rezzi over the edge? Did he know about a stash of money Rezzi had? Julio and his dad were poor. They barely got by. Maybe Mr. Avila might have thought he could use the money to help Julio. Maybe he thought he could give his son a better life. How much was Rezzi's life worth? A poor, sick old man out of contact with any family.

"No," Naomi asserted firmly, "I don't believe it."

"I'll be at your house this afternoon, Naomi," Clay declared. "I'll be there right after your father gets home from work. You can't stop me. I'm going to be telling him all the stuff I found out. I owe him that. He's always been on my side. He's always been straight with me. If I can help his cousin, then I'm gonna do it. You can't stop me, girl. I'll be right there in your living room, and you better just deal with it."

CHAPTER FOUR

Naomi went to her next class. She scarcely heard a word the teacher said. Her thoughts were about Clay's story. She had known Julio Avila almost all her life, though she never got close to him. Few people did. He was a loner with just one parent, a difficult boy with a lot of issues of his own. Julio was the best runner on the Chavez track team, with dreams of going for the Olympic gold one day. That dream was all his father lived for—to see his boy run and win. Mr. Avila was always in the stands, jumping up and down and cheering as Julio crossed the finish line. What Clay was doing made Naomi sick. He'd probably hatched this scheme to help Monte

Esposito. All Clay wanted to do was to get in the good graces of Felix Martinez. To do that, he was ready to accuse poor Mr. Avila of murder.

And yet there was the haunting fear in Naomi's heart. Maybe there was some truth to Clay's accusation.

When Naomi arrived home from school, her father's pickup was in the driveway. She didn't see Clay's Mustang. When Naomi got into the house, her father was pacing back and forth, livid with excitement. "Great news," he cried. "Clay Aguirre texted me. He's coming over. He knows who offed old Rezzi. It had nothing to do with Monte. He's gonna tell me everything. Monte is gonna be off the hook!"

Mr. Martinez stopped pacing and faced Naomi. "I'm telling you, that Clay Aguirre is all right. He's better than my own sons. He cares so much for this family, which ain't even his own. He even goes down into that ravine and questions the losers down there. And he comes up with the truth about what happened with Rezzi. Clay's a great kid. He'll be here any minute, now."

Felix Martinez turned toward the kitchen door, shouting to his wife. "Linda, you got some of those macaroon cookies left? Did you give them all to those stupid women you wasted a day with yesterday? I want to put some out for my friend, Clay."

"Oh Felix, I'm sorry," Mom apologized. "I gave Maria the leftovers."

"Beautiful!" Dad snarled. "Well, get some cookies out of the boxes in the cupboard. And get some soda from the fridge. You hear me, woman? Clay's gonna be here any minute. Clay has the good news on the dude who really offed old Rezzi. It ain't my cousin or his friends. They were trying to blame Monte. Ha! It looks like one of the lowlife bums down there killed the old dude. Those guys down there, they got no conscience. They'll kill somebody for a cigarette."

"Dad," Naomi objected, "I'm not sure about all this. Clay told me he went down into the ravine. But he gave some of the men money for information. Maybe they just made stuff up to, you know, get a few more dollars. I don't trust Clay."

Felix Martinez glared at his daughter. "You don't trust Clay? Let me tell you something, girl. I don't trust your phony friend, Ernie Sandoval. I trust Clay a lot more than I trust the phonies you hang around with at school. Y'hear me? I don't trust the Sandovals. And I sure don't trust the Ibarras, but you and Carmen are thick as thieves. Naomi, Clay Aguirre has got more good in his little finger than all those other phonies have in their whole bodies."

He pulled the window curtain aside. "There he is. There's Clay now." Mr. Martinez rushed to the door, opening it. He grabbed Clay's hand and welcomed him. "Come on in, boy. Hey, you're all right. I can't tell you how much I appreciate this. You're way better than my own blood, and that's a fact. I swear to you boy, I ain't never forgetting this."

Clay smiled broadly. He made a special point of looking at Naomi and smirking. Naomi wanted to go to her room, put on her earphones, and drown out the whole thing with rap music. But she also wanted to know exactly what Clay had to say. She needed to know what he'd tell her father.

"Here's the deal, Mr. Martinez," Clay stated. "I was feeling real bad about Councilman Esposito getting in all this trouble. Then I heard on the TV that they were looking into Rezzi's death. I saw maybe they were trying to stick poor Monte with that too. That was too much for me. I decided I had to do something. So I took a few bucks and some deli sandwiches and soda down to the ravine. I started talking to the guys there. I put out the word. I was ready to reward anybody who could help me find out what really happened to Rezzi that night."

Felix Martinez looked at Naomi scornfully. "You see what a catch this boy is? Nobody in this family done anything like that," he said. He turned back to Clay, "And what did you find out, Clay?"

"Well," Clay went on eagerly, "everybody in the ravine suspected Rezzi had some money hid away. Turns out this guy saw Rezzi struggling with another dude. The dude was choking Rezzi and wanting to know where the money was. Well, the dude gave Rezzi a push. Off he went, down the canyon into the muddy wash, into that fast water."

Felix Martinez's eyes were wild with excitement. "Who was the guy pushed Rezzi over?"

"Name's Avila," Clay reported. "His son is Julio Avila. He's on the track team at Chavez. He's a weird kid. Nobody likes him. Only friend he's got at Chavez is Ernie Sandoval."

"I knew that bum Sandoval was mixed up in this somehow," Felix Martinez commented. "So, who were the guys who told you all this, Clay?"

"One of them is Lonnie Shaw," Clay told him. "He's got a beard. The other one's Mitch Lazaro. He's a fat guy with one leg. He's got one of those fake legs. Lazaro said he saw the whole thing. Shaw heard Rezzi screaming, and he went over to see."

"Clay, *excelente!*" Dad declared in admiration. "To think they were trying to lynch my cousin. They probably woulda succeeded if it wasn't for you."

"Yeah," Clay agreed, smiling broadly as he ate a chocolate chip cookie. "Mitch, he told me everybody down in the ravine hated this dude, Avila. They were really ticked off at him. He'd come down there and try to get on the good side of some of the guys. But he just wanted to rip 'em off. He preyed on those ravine rats. He hung close with Rezzi 'cause of the rumors that the guy had a stash."

"He's a predator, a vulture," Felix Martinez stormed. "I guess Avila got tired of waiting for Rezzi to die. He figured he'd speed things up. Clay, listen. I can't thank you enough for doing all this. I'm gonna call Monte right now and give him the lowdown. They might wanna talk to you, Monte's lawyers. Would that be okay, Clay?"

"Anything I can do I'd be glad to help," Clay replied. "You've always been good to me, Mr. Martinez. I really feel close to this family. I respect you a lot. And you know how I feel about Naomi."

Dad glanced over at Naomi. "Y'hear this? You listening to the boy? He went and helped our family because he cared. That's more than anybody else did. You need to think this over girl. Maybe you been riding the wrong train for a long time."

Clay smiled. "Well, I guess I'll be going now. But if you need any more information or anything, just call me, Mr. Martinez. I'm anxious to help Monte Esposito. He's a good man. He never deserved all this stuff happening to him. The Ibarra people, they got to the grand jury and pushed that indictment through. Those bribery charges, that's just a crock. Is this the way a great public servant like Monte Esposito gets shafted? If so, I don't think decent people will want to run for office anymore."

"Here, here," Dad asserted, again glaring at his daughter. "This girl here, she was passing out flyers for Ibarra. Can you believe that? My own daughter trying to get my cousin out of office. I'm telling you, Clay, there's nothing sharper than the knives your own family sticks in your back when they're disloyal."

After Clay left, Dad got on the phone with his cousin. Then Monte Esposito had his lawyer call the Martinez house. Felix Martinez talked to the lawyer for about ten minutes. He gave him the names of the men who, Clay said, saw Mr. Avila pushing Rezzi over the edge to his death.

Dad was grinning when he finally put down the phone. "We're gonna see some heads roll now," he announced. "And it won't be Monte and his friends. Avila is gonna get what's coming to him."

Naomi's mother was scampering around the kitchen, making her husband's favorite—*chili con queso* casserole. She knew what a terrible mood he had been in, and she was trying to cheer him up somehow. She was chopping green chilies and tomatoes, adding shredded cheese and baking mix. She put in eggs and sour cream, filling the house with lovely aromas.

Naomi joined her mother in the kitchen to help fix dinner. Mom told her, "I know you've broken up with Clay, Naomi. But I'm so grateful to the boy that he found out the truth about that Rezzi's death. I haven't seen your father so happy in days. I'm so thankful for that. It really was a beautiful thing that Clay did."

"Mom," Naomi stated in a soft voice so her father couldn't overhear her, "I don't think anything Clay said was the truth. I think Clay went down there and waved money around. These two guys told him what he wanted to hear. Never mind that the lies are going to cause horrible trouble for an innocent man—Mr. Avila. Clay manufactured the whole thing. He was hoping that, if he did something good for this family, I would maybe go back with him. But I'll never date him again, not ever."

Linda Martinez looked at her daughter, distress on her face. "Just so it made your father a little happier," Mom said. "I don't even care if it's true or not. He's been so sad and angry that I've been afraid. He flies into such rages that I think he'll have a heart attack or a stroke. Then I'll be all alone. If Clay coming here with that story made him smile and laugh for a little while, then I don't ask for more than that."

Naomi didn't say any more. Once again, she felt sorry for her mother. She was so anxious to preserve the status quo, however miserable it was. She didn't even care about the truth anymore. She just wanted Felix Martinez to be appeased, even if that meant throwing an innocent man to the wolves.

Naomi remembered reading a book in sophomore English. Part of the story took place in Siberia, a frozen part of Russia. A group of people were in a sled racing across the bleak frozen land. A pack of hungry wolves were pursuing them, and the sled was moving too slowly with its burden of people. The wolves drew closer. Everyone was terrified. The wolves were about to catch up with them. When they did, they would attack, tearing them all to pieces. Then someone got the idea to lighten the burden in the sled by throwing one of the people off. With one less person, the sled would move faster, and the wolves would have a meal. So one of the people was sacrificed and set upon by the wolves. The sled sped on, and everyone was glad to have been spared. Naomi was reminded of that story now. Linda Martinez did not care who had to be sacrificed. She just wanted peace returned to her house.

Later that evening, at dinner, Felix Martinez was in a good mood, singing the praises of Clay Aguirre. He looked at Zack and said, "Son, except for you, that Clay Aguirre is more family to me than anybody."

Zack smiled and responded, "I like Clay. I always liked him. He's a great guy."

Naomi focused on her *chili con queso*. She thought, if her father gave King Kong a hug, Zack would welcome the gorilla into the house as a pet.

When dinner was over, Naomi was glad to be away from the table and in her room. She called Ernesto and told him everything that had happened.

"Oh brother!" Ernesto groaned. "Poor Julio. The cops will be coming around now hassling his poor father. I don't believe any of that rot Clay is spewing. Mr. Avila isn't a violent person. He's so frail. I can't imagine him even having the strength to attack Rezzi. Besides, he really was Rezzi's friend."

"Ernie," Naomi said, "I'm afraid Clay will be spreading the lies all over school.

He'll be bragging that he solved a big murder mystery and rescued an innocent man—Esposito. When it gets back to Julio, he'll go ballistic."

"Yeah," Ernesto agreed, "if the cops show up at the Avila house and give Julio's father a bad time, Julio's gonna freak."

"You can't believe the stuff my father is saying, Ernie," Naomi went on. "My Dad thinks Clay's now the most wonderful guy in the world for digging up this phony story. Dad's saying that Clay is more family to him than any of us, except for Zack of course. Zack kisses Dad's foot about everything. Oh Ernie, I feel so terrible. Here I was trying to figure out a way to bring my family together for Dad's fiftieth birthday. Now we're more divided than ever." Tears filled Naomi's eyes.

"Babe," Ernesto suggested. "Why don't I come over there right now and pick you up? I don't work at the pizzeria tonight. You don't work at the yogurt shop. So we could just hang out together and . . ."

"Oh no," Naomi interrupted. "If you showed up around here now, I don't know what Dad would do. He's really down on you, Ernie. Clay mentioned how you're Julio Avila's friend. Dad got this horrible look on his face, like you hang with a murderer's son. Dad's in this 'Clay is a great big hero and Ernesto is no good' mode. I just don't want any more trouble."

Naomi felt bad for what she just said. She looked down. "Thanks for offering, Ernie. You don't know how much I'd love to be with you right now. I feel so lonely and isolated in this house. Mom and Zack would appease Dad no matter what it cost anybody. All Dad cares about right now is helping his cousin. I think the only friend I have right now is Brutus."

"I'm sorry, babe," Ernesto sympathized. "Love you."

"See you at school tomorrow," Naomi bid good-bye. "Love you more."

Naomi closed the phone and tried to get some math homework done. Then she heard her parents talking in the living room, and she couldn't concentrate.

"She made a heckuva mistake cutting Clay out of her life," Dad was saying. "So he lost his temper and hit her that one time. Big deal! He didn't mean anything by that. The way I heard it, she was flirting with that jerk Sandoval. That's what ticked Clay off. What guy worth his salt woulda taken that lying down? Just proved how much he cared about her. Clay apologized. He sent her roses. He did everything he could to make up for that one mistake. But she drops him like a hot potato and goes with Sandoval. I don't get it."

"Well, I guess Naomi was shocked when he punched her in the face," Mom countered. "She looked kinda bad . . ."

"So, big deal!" Mr. Martinez stormed. "She wasn't really injured or anything. What guy doesn't get a little rough with his woman?"

"Felix, I don't think Ernesto does," Linda Martinez said softly. "I think he's very gentle."

"That's because he ain't a real man, see?" Felix Martinez snarled in a harsh voice. "His father, he's a wimpy girlie man too. He shouldn't even be teaching in high school. That's a woman's job. If a guy wants to teach, he oughta be teaching in college. That'd be okay. But in high school, they're dealing with kids. They need women. This dude Sandoval, he's not a real man, and neither is his son. They're weak, sissy guys who let the chicks in their lives lead them around. I seen that Maria Sandoval with her husband, and she lets him know what she wants. The guy has no authority in his family."

Naomi listened sadly. "Now our daughter, she's gone for that sappy Ernie Sandoval. She's turned her back on a great kid—Clay Aguirre. You shoulda seen the way he was looking at Naomi. She's breaking his heart. It was enough to make a grown man cry to see the hurt in that kid's eyes. He wants Naomi back. Man, she should be going to him and counting herself lucky to have a real guy." He was silent for a second or two. Naomi figured he was looking hard at his wife. "Linda, you seen the way Clay looks at Naomi, haven't you?"

"Yes," Linda Martinez responded. "I know he loves her. But girls aren't the same today as they were when we were young, Felix. It's a whole new world now. Girls want to be equal. They want the boys they go with to respect them. I've seen Ernie when he picks Naomi up. He holds the door for her and stuff like that. When Clay would pick her up, he'd sit out there in his car and honk the horn for her to come out."

"That's a lot of garbage," Felix Martinez yelled. "Chicks want to be equal? What's that mean? Like we're equal in our marriage? I go to work every day. I slave away with my back hurting and my feet hurting. Then I bring home the money that keeps this joint going. You sit around the house reading magazines and watching TV. Is that equal? You doin' as much to keep this ship afloat as I am? It ain't supposed to be equal. A man has to work twice as hard as his woman. In exchange for that, he's got to have some respect around the house."

"I do respect you, Felix," Mom replied in a small voice. "I try to keep the house clean and fix the meals you like."

"Oh yeah, that's a big thing," Felix Martinez sneered. "Dustin' around the corners every coupla weeks. Dumpin' the clothes in the ritzy washer I paid for. Dryin' 'em in the big modern dryer I paid for. *Big* stuff there. Dishwasher does the dishes. Take me about seven minutes to do all you do around here."

Mr. Martinez extended his hand in the air and shook his head slowly. "But listen, I ain't complaining. I don' mind taking care of you, Linda. You're my wife. I took a vow to take care of you. And I'm gonna do that till my dying day. And that probably ain't far off, me working so hard and having all the grief I got to deal with. I'm almost fifty, very close to the time when my old man kicked the bucket, you know."

"Don't talk like that, Felix," Mrs. Martinez told him, in a sad tone. "You're going to have a good, long life."

In her bedroom, Naomi was shaken. She resented her mother's slavish devotion to her father. Mom was unwilling to assert herself in the least way that might annoy him. Yet she pitied her mother for having such a desperate need to please him.

"Listen," Dad went on, "guy like me's lucky to see fifty-five. But, like I say, you're okay, Linda. Once in a while you make a really nice meal like you did tonight. Really good. You're all right. You respect me, and that means a lot to me. Like I tell you something, and you do it. My old man had a saying. A good wife is somebody who, when her husband says, 'Jump,' she goes, 'How high?' My mother was like that. Dad was the boss, boy. I ain't saying they had this great romantic marriage like some people have. But, boy, Mama listened to Papa."

Naomi sighed so deeply that her whole body seemed to tremble. She walked to the window and looked up at the crescent moon. She remembered her father's parents. Naomi was about eight when her grandfather died. She recalled a gruff, unsmiling man. He was very much like her own father, perhaps even a little tougher. Naomi's grandmother was still alive. She had moved to a retirement community in Florida and had done a lot of traveling. She'd been all over the world. She sent postcards of herself standing at the wall of China and in front of the pyramids in Egypt. Yet Naomi thought her grandmother looked very happy in those pictures from Egypt and China.

Naomi wondered whether the police had already arrived at the small Avila home. Were they questioning Mr. Avila about the death of Rezzi? She thought the old man would be shocked at the news that he was a suspect. Probably they wouldn't even tell him he was a suspect. They'd just ask him some questions. If he didn't have the right answers, they'd read him his rights. Naomi wiped tears from her eyes. She was crying for Julio, for his dad, for her mother, and for herself.

CHAPTER FIVE

The next morning, Friday, Naomi biked to school with her math homework tucked into her backpack. She'd finally understood all of it, thanks to Yvette Ozono, who was helping her. Yvette was so good in math she could make the toughest problems seem easy. Naomi now thought she had an outside chance of getting an A in math, thanks to Yvette.

As Naomi parked her bike, she saw Ernesto Sandoval and Abel Ruiz looking around in a worked-up state.

"Hey you guys, what's up?" Naomi called to them.

Ernesto looked very upset. "Julio's looking for Clay Aguirre, Naomi. He's fighting mad. He called me up and said the cops were at his place last night. They were asking his dad about where he was the night Rezzi was killed. They wanted to know how he knew Rezzi. Things like that. And we all know where that's coming from."

"Oh no!" Naomi cried.

"Clay's been telling everybody that Mr. Avila pushed Rezzi over the edge," Abel added. "He said Julio's dad did it to cover up the theft. Now Julio wants to take Clay apart. We're trying to find Julio before he takes on Clay and gets his clock cleaned."

Behind Cesar Chavez High School was a vacant field that guys occasionally used to settle scores. But when Ernesto and Abel checked it out, they didn't find Julio or Clay. As they walked back on campus, loud voices rang out from behind the science building. It was still early, and no teachers had arrived in the area. But a few students were around.

"Big fight breakin' out!" a boy yelled.

Ernesto and Abel rushed behind the science building to see Julio screaming at Clay Aguirre.

"You lied, you filthy snake!" Julio yelled. "You sent the cops after my dad on a lie. My father never took a penny from Rezzi. Rezzi didn't have no money. Most he ever had was a coupla dollars!"

"I know what those dudes told me," Clay taunted. "Rezzi had a lot of money with those pictures and letters. When your old man got a hold of it, he had to kill Rezzi to cover things up. The one dude saw your father push Rezzi over the edge. And the other guy heard Rezzi screamin' all the way down."

"That's all a rotten lie!" Julio shouted. "I'm takin' you out, Aguirre. This is gonna kill my dad. You're not gettin' away with it!"

"He's got a switchblade," Abel gasped.

Ernesto and Abel lunged at Julio, stopping him before he could reach Clay. They got Julio on the ground, and Ernesto yanked his arm behind his back. Abel took the switchblade. It hadn't been snapped open. Abel hurled it over the school fence into the brush of a vacant lot.

"Calm down, man!" Ernesto ordered Julio. "Don't do this! You'll ruin your whole life. It ain't worth it man. Your father's gonna be okay. It's all lies, and he'll be cleared. If you do something stupid like this man, *that'll* kill your dad for sure."

"You're a dirty gangbanger," Clay yelled. "Trying to pull a knife on me. You oughta be thrown out of school right now, you little creep."

"What're you talking about?" Ernesto demanded. Ernesto jumped to his feet and took a step toward Clay, glaring at him. "He didn't have no knife."

Julio got slowly to his feet. He was trembling with rage and fear. He had begun to understand the enormity of what he'd almost done.

"He had a blade," Clay insisted. "You guys saw it!"

"No, he didn't," Abel declared. "He didn't have no blade. We're witnesses."

Clay was ashen. "Ruiz, you tossed the switchblade over the fence," he said. "I saw you take it from him and toss it."

"*You* had the switchblade, Aguirre," Ernesto told him in a hard, cold voice. "*You* got scared when you saw us coming. *You* tossed it there into the brush in that vacant field. You're in big trouble, Aguirre, bringing a blade onto campus. You might be expelled."

"*You're lying!*" Clay Aguirre gasped. He couldn't believe what Ernesto Sandoval and Abel Ruiz were doing. But he was terrified they'd make their accusation stick. Clay looked around at the few other students standing at a distance. No one was going to help him out. It was his word against that of Ernesto and Abel. So, in a shaky voice, Clay admitted, "I guess there wasn't any switchblade. It was just a trick the sun was playing."

"I guess that's right," Ernesto confirmed.

"Yeah," Abel added. "Just the sunlight."

"Get outta here, Aguirre," Ernesto commanded. "I'm warning you. *Just move.*"

For the first time in his life, Clay Aguirre was afraid of Ernesto Sandoval. He hurried away as fast as he could.

Abel dashed over to the vacant field and retrieved the closed switchblade. School didn't start for another twenty minutes. He jumped on his bike, riding for home. He'd be back without the blade in time for the first bell.

Ernesto grabbed the front of Julio's shirt. "Man, don't you *ever* bring anything like that on campus again. Y'hear me? I'm not kidding you, Julio. I know you're upset for your dad, but that was crazy stupid. Y'hear me? I had your back this one time, but you pull something like this again, and I swear I'll turn you in."

"You shoulda seen my old man last night when the cops came," Julio murmured in a broken voice. "He was shakin' all over. He's got a weak heart. He's smoked cigarettes all his life. He hasn't taken care of himself. Just the shock of seeing two cops at the door out there last night, just that coulda taken him out. And it's all lies. My father wasn't even there when Rezzi went over the side. He was comin' in the morning to pick him up to take him down to the DA's office. When Pop got to the ravine, they were recovering the body."

Julio had been talking with his face turned away, talking almost to himself. Now he turned to look Ernesto in the eyes. "Why'd Aguirre do that? What's my father ever done to him? What have I ever done to him?"

"I know, man," Ernesto sympathized, "but that's no excuse to bring a blade on campus."

"Ernie, my old man never got any breaks," Julio went on, as if he never heard Ernesto. "His whole life has been the pits. I wanted to give him something so he could die happy. I think I'm good enough to win some medals. I want to give him that. When he's lying in his coffin, I promised him I'd pin my medal on his chest. Why'd Aguirre want to take that away from us?" Ernesto had never seen Julio so emotional. He sounded as though he was cracking up.

"Look man," Ernesto advised. "Go home. Tell your dad to call into the office that you're sick, okay? It's gonna be okay, Julio. I promise you."

Naomi stood at a distance, watching sadly.

"If this kills my dad, I'm getting Aguirre," Julio swore. "In some dark alley, I'm gonna be there behind him."

"Don't talk like that, man," Ernesto commanded. "You think that's what your father wants for his only son? To end up a murderer living out his life in a cage?"

Julio's dark eyes were wet with what looked like tears of rage. Naomi walked over to him, put her arms around him, and gave him a hug. "I hate Clay Aguirre so much, Julio," she told him. "I hate what he did. I'm ashamed that I ever dated him."

Naomi took Julio by the shoulders and held him at arms' length. "Julio," she asked, "I was wondering about the two guys Clay was talking about. Did you ever hear your father mention their names? Lonnie Shaw? Mitch Lazaro?"

Julio's eyes widened. "Lazaro goes around pretending he has one leg, but he doesn't. He just gets more handouts from doing that. Yeah, I heard of him and that other guy, Shaw. He's got a dirty beard. They hang together. They're cheats and liars. One lies, and the other one swears to it. There's bad blood between them and my father. Once they mugged some guys in the ravine who were drinking. My dad called the cops on them. One time my dad and Rezzi caught them stealing a watch. Dad and Rezzi, they whipped their butts."

Ernesto saw where Naomi was going with her question. "So," he suggested, "they not only had Clay's money as a motive to lie, but they hate your dad. They thought this would be a good way of getting back at him. Look, Julio, go home. After school, me and Abel and Naomi will come over to your place and talk to your dad. Go home and tell your dad to take it easy. It's gonna be okay. My uncle—Uncle Arturo— he's a lawyer. He'll help the cops get this sorted out."

By this time, Julio had calmed down. "Okay, Ernie," he mumbled. "Uh . . . thanks. Hey man, tell Abel thanks too. Okay? Thanks for everything."

After school, Ernesto, Abel, and Naomi all got into Ernie's Volvo. They headed for the small apartment where Julio and his father lived. It was a three-room unit behind a larger apartment.

When Julio saw the Volvo, he opened the front door. "It's pretty messy in here," he warned.

"That's okay," Ernesto said. "My friend Carmen's dating a dude named Paul

Morales. We all love the guy, but he lives in a bachelor pad. It's a rat's nest. You gotta wade through the mess if you want to visit."

"My mom's a neat freak," Abel remarked. "She drives me crazy. If a tiny piece of wrapping paper falls on the floor, she comes running to get it. When I go away to culinary school, I'm gonna live like a pig. I'm givin' in to my inner slob."

Mr. Avila was slumped in an old, overstuffed chair. A bottle of whiskey stood on the floor near his chair. He was reaching for it, but Julio snatched the bottle away. "You had enougha this, Dad," he told him.

Mr. Avila stared at the three young people in his home. He had seen Ernesto before, running against his son in the track meets. He'd seen the two boys high-fiving each other after a race—like good sports. He'd seen the beautiful girl too. She came to all the track meets. He didn't know Abel, though.

Ernesto pulled up a chair near Mr. Avila, while Abel went to make coffee. "Mr. Avila," Ernesto said, "I'm real sorry about this mess. I'm sorry the cops came around and bummed you out."

Mr. Avila nodded. "Somebody spreading it around that I robbed Rezzi," he sighed, "and then killed him. I never done that. I loved the guy. He was my best friend. He told me to collect his stuff if anything ever happened to him. He said to look for his family and see that they got his pictures and letters. He had no money, just some dollar bills. There was the envelope with the political stuff in it. When I got to the ravine, Rezzi was dead. They was fishing him out. I got his stuff then, like he asked me."

"Can you remember what happened the day he died?" Ernesto asked.

"The cops asked me all that," Mr. Avila answered, shrugging his shoulders. "All I know is he was real upset that those lyin' flyers were going around about Ibarra. Rezzi decided he needed to tell the DA what a crook Monte Esposito was. It was raining that day. It's awful for those homeless guys when it's raining. It's the worst in that muddy place."

Abel brought the coffee. Mr. Avila wrapped his hands around the cup. He didn't seem to mind its being scalding hot. His hands were shaking, but somehow he steadied the cup and took big gulps from it.

"I come in the morning, like I said," Mr. Avila continued, "The paramedics were there already. I didn't know what happened. Somebody told me Rezzi fell or was pushed into the wash. They were going for his body. I felt terrible. I cried like a baby. But I remembered what I'd promised him. I went to his tarp and I got the stuff. Rezzi, he was down on his luck like me, but he was a gentleman. He was always a gentleman."

"Do you remember seeing Lonnie Shaw and Mitch Lazaro there that day?" Ernesto asked. "They were the guys who said they saw you push Rezzi into the wash."

Mr. Avila shook his head, no. "I didn't see 'em that day. Hadn't seen 'em in a while. They didn't hang in the ravine so much then. They had a new place. Rezzi and me gave them a hard time once. We caught 'em stealing from some of the other men. So they started camping behind the thrift store on Washington."

"See," Abel declared, "they weren't even there when Rezzi went over the edge. How could they have seen anything? It was all a lie. They were telling Aguirre what he wanted to hear, for the money."

"Now and then they'd come around," Mr. Avila went on. "But they weren't living there no more."

Mr. Avila looked around at the young people in his apartment. "I'm not proud of some of the things I've done in my life. The fact is I'm probably not proud of anything except this boy of mine. But I never hurt nobody. I been in fights, and I got drunk and worse. But I never harmed nobody. If I ever harmed somebody, Rezzi would have been the last person in the world I would a hurt. He was the closest I ever had to a brother. The day he died, I wept like a baby." He turned with his watery, blood-shot eyes to his son, "Didn't I cry, Julio?"

"Yeah Pop," Julio told him. Julio put his arm around his father's stooped shoulders. "It's okay, Dad. It's gonna be okay."

Ernesto, Abel, and Naomi left the small apartment. On their way to the Volvo, Ernesto said, "You know, after Rezzi died, Mr. Avila gave all that stuff to my dad. Dad gave it to Uncle Arturo. My uncle's been trying to locate the family, Rezzi's family. He wants the family to have the pictures and some stuff Rezzi wrote to his kids, you know, telling them that he loved them. I'm gonna call my Uncle Arturo. I'll ask him if there was anything in Rezzi's letters about him having any money stashed away."

"That's a good idea," Naomi agreed. "Maybe he was stashing some money for his family. Or maybe that was just what people thought. Maybe Lonnie and Mitch suspected that and . . . who knows?"

Abel's eyes narrowed. "Maybe one of them—or both of them—tried to make Rezzi tell where the money was. They told Clay that fishy story about Mr. Avila and Rezzi fighting over the money. But maybe it was them."

Later that day, after school, Ernesto told his dad about what Mr. Avila had said. Luis Sandoval called his brother, but Arturo was out; so he left a message. Mr. Sandoval said he wanted to ask about Rezzi's last effects and that it was really important.

In the morning, right after breakfast, Uncle Arturo called Mr. Sandoval back. Ernesto was nearby and overheard one end of the conversation.

"Arturo," Luis began, after exchanging greetings, "Ernesto suggested I call you. I was wondering if Rezzi—David Juarez— referred to any money in the letters he wrote for his children. There were rumors that he had money stashed away in the ravine somewhere."

Uncle Arturo was silent for a few moments; so Luis felt he had to explain himself. "*Mi hermano*, some people are saying Rezzi had some money stashed, you know, for his family. Maybe when Rezzi drank too much, he talked about it to the wrong people. Guys like him sometimes run off at the mouth when they're drunk. But Mr. Avila, he said he didn't find any money under Rezzi's tarp where the other stuff was—"

"Yes Luis," Arturo interrupted. "In several letters, David Juarez told his children about some money. He'd had saved a little more than a thousand dollars in denominations of one hundred dollar bills. He told the children they could have this money. It wasn't much, he said, but it would be about three hundred and fifty for each child. He had three children. Two boys and a girl. Rezzi said he wrote his initials on all the bills. He said he hoped that, before they spent the money, they would look at those initials and say a prayer for him."

"But there was no money found under the tarp," Luis said. "That's what Mr. Avila said."

"In two of the letters," Arturo explained, "Mr. Juarez instructed his children that he had sewn a pouch on the inside of his shirt. He always wore the same shirt. He would wash it in the Laundromat. Then he'd put it back on after it came from the dryer. He told the children that they should ask whoever finds his body to look for the money in the pouch and save it for his children. Mr. Juarez didn't want to leave his precious bequest to his children under the tarp with the other things."

"So when the body was taken from the wash . . . ?" Luis asked.

"I later told the police about the reference to the pouch in the letters," Arturo responded. "They said a pouch was sewn into his shirt all right, but it had been ripped open. No money was recovered."

"So maybe the money was washed out of the pouch in the fast-moving water down there in the wash?" Mr. Sandoval suggested.

"Maybe," his brother replied. "Or maybe there was a struggle with somebody before he went over the edge. Maybe whoever he fought with took the money."

"*Gracias, mi hermano*, Arturo," Luis said.

Arturo kept Luis on the line for a few minutes. Arturo, always the lawyer, lectured his brother on the law before hanging up.

By the end of the call, Luis Sandoval looked very serious. "*Mi hijo*," he said to Ernesto, "sometimes bad men tell very elaborate stories about the crimes of someone else. But they are really describing their own actions. Clay Aguirre went into the ravine and offered money. He asked who could help solve the mystery of Rezzi's death. If someone in that ravine had guilty knowledge of what really happened that night, he might have come forward. He—or they—might have used the opportunity to point the finger of guilt at someone else."

"Dad," Ernesto suggested, "you got a friend down at the police station. Could you tell him about this? Maybe Lazaro or Shaw still has some of the money. It's just a guess. But maybe the police could go there and check those guys out."

Luis Sandoval smiled. "David Juarez was down on his luck, but he was not *estúpido*. His initials are on every one of those bills. I'll make the phone call, *mi hijo*."

Ernesto didn't want to call Julio, He couldn't say yet that Shaw and Lazaro were probably the ones who took the money. He couldn't say for sure that Julio's dad was off the hook. Ernesto didn't know any of that yet.

At school on Monday, when Ernesto saw Clay Aguirre, he hailed him. Clay looked alarmed. After the encounter with Julio, Clay looked at Ernesto in a different way. Ernesto had a dark side that Clay had never seen before. Now he was cautious.

"Yeah man. What?" Clay asked nervously.

Ernesto didn't like talking with Clay. He never did. But he asked his question in as calm a tone as he could. "You went down there to the ravine to ask about Rezzi's death man, right? How'd you end up talking to Shaw and Lazaro?"

"Uh," Clay stuttered, "you know, the word spread that a kid came down asking questions about Rezzi's death. I had some folded green for the right answers. They approached me then. They seemed real eager to talk."

"Man, lissen up," Ernesto pressed. "Did you sort of let 'em know you were looking for a way to clear Monte Esposito?"

"Well," Clay conceded, "I might have said something about that poor innocent guy being railroaded for something he didn't do. You know . . ."

"Who mentioned Mr. Avila first?" Ernesto asked.

"Uh well," Clay explained, "we got to talking. Lazaro goes, 'You know who went through the dead guy's stuff, don't you? That creep Avila.' Then they sorta told me the story."

Ernesto's heart raced. It was beginning to look like Rezzi was taken out by people as down on their luck as he was. They were people even lower than Monte Esposito.

CHAPTER SIX

At the track meet against Hillsdale on Tuesday, Ernesto wasn't sure the best runner, Julio Avila, would even show up. Rumors ran wild all over school that Julio's father was in serious trouble. Clay Aguirre had spread the rumors. Coach Gus Muñoz didn't know all the details, but he was worried. Julio had missed one practice already, and he wasn't answering his phone.

Muñoz glanced into the stands where Mr. Avila usually sat, ready to cheer for his son. But he didn't see the man. Coach Muñoz felt sorry that the Chavez Cougars might be missing their best runner, but he felt even sorrier for what the family was going through. He knew that Mr. Avila was just a few dollars away from being a street person. Julio had a job at the supermarket bagging groceries. That paycheck, plus the old man's Social Security check, was what kept them going.

Ernesto was warming up. He hadn't heard anything about the investigation into Rezzi's death. He had his doubts about Julio's showing up for the meet. Ernesto had become the second best runner on the team. Without Julio Avila, the team would depend on him to save the Chavez Cougars pride. Ernesto feared that, without Julio, Chavez would resume its dismal record of losing every meet.

Ernesto stood near the stands with Naomi. "I tried calling Julio all day yesterday," Ernesto told her. "No luck. I kept getting voice mail."

As they waited, Clay Aguirre came along with Mira Nuñez. Ordinarily, Clay would have made a snide remark about Mr. Avila's probably being in the slammer. But

Ernesto frightened him the other day. He'd always thought Ernesto was a wimp. Now he wasn't so sure.

Naomi looked away as Clay and Mira walked by. When she first broke up with Clay, she'd had a few regrets. A few times, right after their breakup, she even considered forgiving him and trying to start over. She had had a fantasy. Maybe Clay Aguirre would take an anger management class and become a different person. But now Clay had tried to shift blame for Rezzi's death onto Mr. Avila. Naomi's last shred of respect for him was gone. She didn't even want to look at him.

"Well," Ernesto declared, "it looks like Julio isn't coming to school today. I don't know what happened."

"Yeah," Naomi agreed sadly. But then she pointed. "Ernie! Look! Isn't that Julio coming up on his motorcycle?"

Ernesto blinked. Julio Avila drove a ratty old motorcycle that had been headed for the junkyard. He'd bought it cheap and refurbished it. Now it roared into the Chavez parking lot. Julio jumped off and came toward Ernesto and Naomi. He walked right past Clay without even looking at him. He grinned at Ernesto and announced, "Hey man, I'm gonna win the hundred meter and the two hundred. Just watch me go. I hope you don't have to eat too much dust, Ernie."

Ernesto grinned too. "It'll be my pleasure, dude," he replied.

"Julio," Naomi asked anxiously, "is everything—"

"Yeah, it's okay now," Julio nodded. "The cops searched Lonnie Shaw's stuff and Lazaro's. They had a couple hundred dollars left. They didn't know Rezzi had initialed his money. The cops got them red-handed. They're saying they argued with Rezzi and stole his money. They're not admitting yet to pushing him off the edge. But it looks like that's what they did. After they robbed him, they didn't want him to live to tell about it. I think they're looking at murder charges."

Ernesto grabbed Julio and gave him a hug. "Man," Ernesto told him, "you made my day."

"Ernie," Julio said, his voice suddenly choked with emotion, "what you did the other day . . . tackling me and stopping me from . . . you, know. You and Abel. I'll never forget what you guys did for me. Never."

"And now you're gonna make me look bad in the track meet?" Ernesto protested, laughing.

Both boys were laughing when Clay skulked away.

Julio was brilliant in the track meet. His father arrived a little late. But his enthusiasm was greater than ever. When Julio won the hundred and two hundred meter races, he was jumping so high his feet seemed to leave the ground. Ernesto came in second. But, as usual, Ernesto helped lead the Chavez relay team to victory. Chavez won the meet.

After school on Wednesday, Naomi was doing an earlier shift than usual. Ernesto drove her right to work at Chill Out. He planned to pick her up at seven and take her home. Sherry at Chill Out had offered to drive Naomi home. But both Ernesto and Naomi treasured the time together driving home, short as it was.

Naomi's shift ended, and she got in Ernesto's car. He asked her, "You think it would be okay if I stopped in your house tonight for a few minutes? I know your dad doesn't like me much. But I could scratch Brutus behind the ears and say hi to your mom."

"Dad's cooled down a lot since Monte's been cleared for Rezzi's death, Ernie," Naomi responded. "I guess it'd be okay."

"Well, maybe I could sort of go in then," Ernesto said. He didn't want Mr. Martinez to get into the habit of being too hostile to him. That could put a serious hurt on his relationship with Naomi. He wanted at least a polite connection with Naomi's father.

"Ernie," Naomi said, suddenly brightening. "I know what you could do. You know that new office building at the end of Washington? That six-story place they're building? Dad's working the crane there to lift up supplies. You could sorta comment on what a tricky operation that must be. You know, ask isn't he scared of going up there and stuff. Give him the chance to brag a little."

"Yeah," Ernesto said. "I've seen that building. It must be really cool working on it."

"You might say you noticed his pickup there. You could ask if he's working there," Naomi suggested. "I know that's kinda sneaky but . . ."

"Listen, whatever works," Ernesto declared. "I'm desperate. It's no fun being the bad guy to your babe's father."

Ernesto came into the house. Brutus barked a friendly greeting and came over for his head scratch. Ernesto obliged him. After that, things turned icy.

Felix Martinez was sitting in his favorite chair. When he spotted Ernesto, he ignored him. But he said to Naomi, "Hey, look what the cat dragged in. Did we forget to lock the door again?" He glared at Ernesto. "So, Sandoval," he sneered, "to what do we owe the misfortune of you coming in here?"

Ernesto had not expected such a hostile reception. For a second, he was knocked off his plan. "Good evening, Mr. Martinez," he stammered. "Hey, I saw your pickup down at the Horizon building site the other day. That's a big project. You operating the crane there, I suppose? Must be real tricky business. I sure wouldn't want to be operating a rig like that."

Felix Martinez was silent for a few seconds. Then he replied. "Yeah, I'm on the crane there. You gotta get the building materials way up there for the guys to work on the top floors. It ain't easy. I'll tell you that. You screw up there, and you have bodies in the street. They won't let nobody but me operate the crane. Some of those youngbloods down there, they're anxious for a crack at it. But the boss ain't listening. I never had no accident with the crane, and they'd like to keep it that way."

"You must be very good at it, Mr. Martinez," Ernesto told him. "That's no small achievement." Ernesto hated himself for being such a bootlicker, but he had no choice. Of course, it *was* true that Felix Martinez was the bomb as a crane operator. That was no lie.

Felix Martinez stared at Ernesto. Then he looked at his daughter. "What's with this guy?" he asked Naomi.

"Nothing, Daddy," Naomi responded. "We got to talking about the Horizon building. Ernie was saying how hard it must be to get people up there to work. He's just impressed with people who do those kinds of jobs."

"Yeah," Mr. Martinez agreed, "it's dangerous working with the heavy machinery and stuff. Not sissy stuff like your pencil pushers do and that kind of work. First of the year, we're goin' downtown. Gonna be a thirty-story hotel on the beach where the rich folks'll go. That'll be really fun."

He paused then and changed the subject. "Hey Sandoval, did you hear about those jackals trying to get my cousin on a trumped-up murder charge. They got skunked. Turns out some creeps right down there in the ravine pushed Rezzi over the edge."

"I heard that," Ernesto replied. "It's great when justice is done, and the innocent walk away."

"Thanks to Clay Aguirre," Mr. Martinez declared, "my cousin ain't in cuffs right now. That kid went down into the ravine. He got the skinny on what was going on. Clay blew the case wide open." The man's eyes were glowing.

Ernesto didn't say anything, but Naomi spoke up. "Daddy, you know how Clay said Mr. Avila had pushed Rezzi over the edge?

Well, Ernesto asked his dad to call his Uncle Arturo. He's got Rezzi's papers, and he's trying to contact Rezzi's family. By reading Rezzi's letters, he found out Rezzi had about a thousand dollars. He was saving it for his kids. He initialed every hundred dollar bill so his kids would remember him."

Naomi's father glanced from her to Ernesto and back. "Well, the police found some of those initialed bills on these two guys, Lonnie Shaw and Mitch Lazaro. Turns out *they* robbed Rezzi. They probably pushed him into the wash to hide their crime. What's really nice is that Clay came up with the names of those guys. Then Ernesto's uncle took it the rest of the way. Now the real criminals will have to pay for what they did. And your Cousin Monte is cleared."

Felix Martinez took all that in. Then he started a tirade. "I think those guys down in the ravine are all criminals. What kinda men don't work and lay around under tarps all day? I'd run them all out outta there. I'd bulldoze that whole place down there. Tell those bums to stop hiding behind their phony addictions, that's what I say."

Naomi's father truly did not understand why the guys in the ravine were homeless. "What's with them anyway? When I was a kid, there weren't a bunch of bums living in ravines and behind thrift stores. Nobody walked the streets asking for handouts. I say the devil take 'em all. If they won't work, throw them in jail, Get them on a chain gang, breaking up rocks or something."

Ernesto breathed a sigh of relief. Mr. Martinez was aiming his bad temper at a different target. The heat was off Ernesto. He felt like a coward to be happy while Naomi's father was ranting against the poor guys in the ravine. But Ernesto couldn't help the feeling of relief.

Naomi shot Ernesto a quick smile. She lived here. She knew the drill. Dad would be angry with Mom for messing up dinner.

Maybe she added too much or too little sea-
soning. He'd start ranting about the lousy
food he gets served in his own house. Then
the nightly news would come on. Dad
would grow furious at the politicians. Or he
wouldn't like the spin the anchorpeople
were putting on the news. Mom would no
longer be the target. The family would be
thankful he had somebody else to be angry
with. They learned to hope for other targets.
Of course, they preferred people who didn't
even know that Felix Martinez hated them.

Naomi went outside with Ernesto and
kissed him good-bye. "It's cool now, babe,"
she told him. "See you at school
tomorrow."

Ernesto gave Naomi a long hug and a
kiss. Then he drove off in the Volvo, hum-
ming a pop tune.

Naomi went to her room and down-
loaded the album Oscar Perez had just put
out. It featured a solo by her brother
Orlando. Naomi had already listened to it.
It had given her chills, it was so beautiful.

Orlando sang a traditional Mexican folk song. Naomi knew her father loved traditional Mexican music, mostly from Veracruz. Naomi went out to the living room, where her father was still sitting. "Dad, you gotta listen to this song. It's so cool," she said.

"What you call cool ain't something I usually want to listen to, Naomi," Dad responded in a disgruntled voice.

"Just listen to it, Dad," Naomi urged him. "It's a folk ballad from Veracruz."

As Orlando's voice filled the room, Naomi saw her father's eyes brighten. It was the kind of music he listened to and loved as a young man. He enjoyed the wailing, heartfelt ballads of love and loss and heartbreak. Felix Martinez began to smile. When the song was finished, he said, "Yeah, that was great. Where'd you get that, Naomi? Some old Mexican group where all the guys are dead? They sang good like that maybe thirty, forty years ago. Now all those great singers are either dead or dodderin' around in nursing homes."

"No Dad, these are young guys from Los Angeles," Naomi told him. "They're rediscovering their roots."

"Yeah?" Felix Martinez asked, his expression still pleasant. "That's good. Most of the new music is rotten, even the Mexican stuff. I seen this Mexican dude on TV the other night. He was hoppin' around like a grasshopper. Sounded like a girl. But this guy here, the one you played, that's a macho man. That's my kind of guy."

Naomi felt numb all over. She longed to tell her father the truth. This wonderful singer was his son, his firstborn son, Orlando Martinez. But she didn't dare. She thought that would just trigger an explosion of rage. Dad would feel tricked, deceived. He'd feel as though Naomi had deliberately made a fool of him.

"So what's this guy's name," Dad asked.

"I didn't get that, Dad. I'll find out," Naomi replied.

"Yeah, you do that," he insisted. "He's a real good singer. Reminds me of when I was a young guy. All the music was like that. Now everything's gone to the dogs."

Mrs. Martinez popped her head through the kitchen doorway. She glared at Naomi, her eyes wide. Naomi hurried to join her in the kitchen.

"Naomi! That song," Mom whispered. "Didn't he recognize Orlando's voice?"

"No Mom," Naomi answered. "Orlando never sang much around here." Naomi had played the song over and over for her mother when Dad was at work. Hearing it made her feel closer to her missing son.

"You were taking a big risk that he would recognize Orlando's voice," Mom advised.

"No, I knew he wouldn't," Naomi objected in a hushed voice. "He thinks Orlando and Manny are big failures anyway. He wouldn't dream that Orlando could be singing a song on an album."

Naomi had to tell her mother about her call to Orlando. "Oh Mom, I phoned Orlando. I told him how depressed Dad was about turning fifty. I told my brother how wonderful it would be if the family came together for Dad's birthday. Dad wouldn't admit how much he misses the boys. But I know he does. I think that's behind all his bitterness."

"What did Orlando say?" Mom asked.

"He said he'd do anything I asked if I thought it would help," Naomi responded. "Orlando loves Dad. So does Manny. There's been a lot of bitterness I know. But when the boys were younger, they had such great times with Dad. They were always together fishing, roughing it in the mountains. I remember when it snowed in the mountains. Dad would pull that sled up the slope a hundred times so the boys could sled down. I remember Dad laughing a lot in those days. We were happy a lot of times, weren't we, Mom?"

Linda Martinez nodded. "Yes, we were happy when you kids were young. Your father was the boss, and everybody knew it. Nobody crossed him, and that pleased him. He was the big leader. He made all the decisions. Then Orlando and Manny got minds of their own. And you . . . did stuff like campaign for Mr. Ibarra against his cousin."

"Mom, I had to do that," Naomi insisted. "Emilio Ibarra is already doing so many good things for the *barrio*. We needed him. I couldn't go against my own conscience."

"I know Naomi," Mrs. Martinez nodded yes. "You have every right to be your own person, honey. But to your father it was just one more sign that what he said didn't matter anymore. Felix is wrong in thinking he can control his grown children. But now he feels like an old king. All his once faithful subjects are abandoning him. When he was a young married man, he imagined how it'd be when he grew old, He'd be surrounded by his children and grandchildren. They would all show him the respect he feels entitled to. Now two of his children are gone. The perfect Mexican family he dreamed of isn't happening."

"That's why I want to get our family together again, Mom," Naomi insisted. "I know Orlando will cooperate, and Manny will follow him."

"But how?" Mrs. Martinez asked. "Your father's so stubborn and unforgiving. He would want for Orlando to apologize. He would want for the boys to ask his forgiveness for the terrible way they behaved. When he first threw them out of the house, he expected they would come back almost at once. He thought they'd be on bended knees, begging to be forgiven. When that didn't happen, his anger hardened into bitterness and hatred."

"But Mom," Naomi protested, "he's still a father. He still loves them deep down."

Mom shook her head in fear. "I shudder to think of what Felix would do if he saw the boys coming through the front door. I don't know what he would do. I was even afraid when Ernesto came in tonight. I thought Felix would throw him out. But Ernesto, he's so gentle and nice that he calms your father down. He's not like Orlando. Your brother is almost as bad as Felix. In his heart and soul burn the same fires that burn in your father's heart. How can they come together?"

Naomi put her arms around her mother and kissed her on the cheek. "There's a way, Mom, and I'll find it," she vowed.

CHAPTER SEVEN

A few days later, Naomi found her brother Zack in the living room, watching TV. Dad wasn't home from work yet.

"We gotta do something for Dad on his fiftieth birthday," she announced.

Zack frowned. His dad had given him a lecture on life just the other day. Zack was still taking classes at the community college and hating every minute of it. He was trying to talk his father into getting him into construction, even if only as a gofer. But Felix Martinez refused. "Boy," he told Zack, "I been breakin' my back for thirty years doin' this kind of work. My back feels like it's busted. The doctors can't do nothin' for me but give me stupid pills that make me sick. I've fallen and fractured bones. I was almost killed once or twice."

Mr. Martinez was firm on the subject. "I want something better for you. I don't want you to end up like me. I'm a broken-down fifty-year-old man with the busted, aching body of a seventy-five-year-old. You get your AA degree from the community college. Then you go on to the state school. Find something you like there. I got two sons who want nothing to do with me. That makes you my only son, Zack. I want something good for you."

That lecture was still ringing in Zack's ears. He switched off the TV and spoke to Naomi. "I don't think Dad wants to be reminded about turning fifty. I think he'd just rather let the day go by without any fuss. He told me he don't want any gifts, nothing. He said he just wants to get together with the guys at work and drink a lot of beer. That's how he wants to celebrate his birthday."

"Zack," Naomi insisted, "we're gonna do something big for Dad. We're gonna show him how much we love him."

"I don't know," Zack objected. "Fifty is really old. I think Dad is afraid of dying pretty soon."

"Don't be silly," Naomi said. "Fifty isn't old. People live into their eighties these days. They still have fun and enjoy life. Come on, Zack. Don't be like this. We're going to have a big party for Dad. I was thinking about contacting all his cronies so they could come. You know, the guys at work that he likes, Eppy, Pogo, Roto. I was thinking about having the party at Hortencia's. She's got that big place, and she'll open up the patio area. It'll fit a lot of people. Dad loves *tamales*. She'll make them and *enchiladas*, guacamole, *nachos*— all the stuff Dad is crazy about. It'll be a big bash."

"Dad doesn't even like Hortencia, 'cause she's a Sandoval," Zack pointed out. "She's Luis Sandoval's sister. Besides, she let them have that big Ibarra rally there. That burned Dad up."

"Zack," Naomi groaned, "I'm dating Ernie Sandoval. Dad's learned to live with that. He's always liked Hortencia as a person. There's not a week goes by that he doesn't stop by there and get *tamales*. Hortencia would decorate the place for us. She'd bring out all the pretty pottery and the paintings. We could hang colorful streamers from the beams. It'd be great."

Zack still didn't seem persuaded. Naomi kept trying. "And the Oscar Perez band would come down to perform. I played one of the songs from their new album, and Dad loved it. He got all teary-eyed. They play a lot of traditional Mexican ballads from Veracruz. They do rock and reggae too, but we'd ask them to stick with the music Dad enjoys."

"I don't know," Zack whined. "Dad seems pretty set on not doing anything for his birthday. He said it would just remind him how old he is."

"You know what, Zack?" Naomi declared. "Dad likes to talk like that to make us all feel bad. He wants us all to think that he's unloved and unappreciated. Then he can sit around and sulk all day. He can have his own little twenty-four-seven pity party. But that's not gonna happen. Dad's going to have a wonderful birthday party. It'll be just like you'd have for somebody who's big and important. He's our dad, Zack. He's taken good care of us, and he *has* worked really hard. I'm going to talk to Hortencia to get things rolling."

Zack's brow was furrowed with worry. "Naomi," he cautioned, "I don't think you better do that. Dad might get so mad he wouldn't even come to his own party."

"Let's see," Naomi began, ignoring her brother. She went over to the desk and took a yellow pad and pen out of the drawer. Sitting at the desk, she started her to-do list. "I gotta list the names of the guys Dad likes down at the job. Eppy, Pogo, Roto, and their wives, of course. I'm listing some of the guys Dad's known all his life, his drinking pals."

She paused a few seconds, tapping the pen on the pad. "Know what?" she asked. "I'm even gonna invite Monte Esposito. Monte's invited Dad to a lot of big parties, and Dad loves the guy. It's only right Monte and his wife Nora come. It'd be fun for Monte to see how many people love and respect our dad too. Monte has always thought Dad was a nobody. He's always thought Dad's only taste of the good life was because of his cousin's generosity. Now he'll see Dad's loved by a lot of friends."

"Who's gonna pay for all this?" Zack asked, switching the TV back on.

"I've been saving my Christmas and birthday gifts from Grandma," Naomi explained. "And Mom's saved a lot of the grocery money Dad gave her over the years. She's a very thrifty shopper. Hortencia will cut us a deal too."

"You mean Mom is in favor of this?" Zack asked, unbelieving.

"Yeah Zack," Naomi assured her brother. "Mom loves Dad, and he loves her. I know Dad gives her a hard time sometimes, but they love each other. You knew that, didn't you?"

"I guess so," Zack replied, uncertain.

Naomi put her pen down and spoke to her brother. "Zack, if I tell you a great big secret, will you promise you won't tell Dad? Will you absolutely, totally promise you won't say a word to Dad about it? Will you swear you won't tell?"

Zack looked upset but kept staring at the television. "What is it?" he asked.

"I can't tell you until you promise you won't say anything about it to Dad," Naomi insisted.

"Naomi, I don't keep secrets from Dad," Zack replied in a conflicted voice.

"But Zack," Naomi objected, "this is something we're doing *for* Dad. This would be the greatest gift Dad ever got in his entire life. But I can't tell you about it unless you promise to keep it a secret no matter what. Okay, Zack?"

"Okay, I guess," Zack promised nervously. "I won't tell." But he didn't take his eyes off the television screen.

"You swear you won't?" Naomi pressed him.

"Yeah, I swear," Zack said, looking miserable.

"Zack," Naomi said excitedly, "I'm going to bring Orlando and Manny to Dad's birthday party."

Zack's head snapped around in Naomi's direction. His eyes grew so large they seemed to fill his entire face. He looked shaken. "Naomi! You can't spring something like that on Dad! He'd be furious!"

"Zack," his sister explained, "Dad is aching inside every day for his sons. He's got too much pride to ever reach out to them. But what if I engineered this, and Orlando and Manny came? You know, what if I could get Orlando to apologize. I think it would be the happiest day of Dad's life."

"Naomi, you gotta promise me never to tell Dad that I knew about this beforehand. Okay?" Zack pleaded.

"Yeah, sure," Naomi agreed. "If Dad asks, I'll tell him you knew nothing about it. But, oh Zack, what gift could mean more to our Dad than getting his boys back? He'd have the family together again. Orlando and Manny wouldn't be enemies anymore. It would be such a wonderful thing, Zack. I want to do this for Mom and for my brothers, but especially for Dad. I think losing his boys has made him old before his time."

Naomi sat back in the chair by the desk. "Remember years ago when we'd all go to those tailgate parties? We did that whenever the Chargers were playing. Dad would be on top of the world with his three sons. All you guys would be in Charger jerseys. Don't you notice that, since Orlando and Manny are gone, we haven't been to one Charger game?"

"Yeah," Zack acknowledged. He still seemed nervous about the whole party idea.

But Naomi believed she had convinced him to keep quiet about it.

After school the next day, Naomi went over to Hortencia's for a *tamale*. Hortencia was her usual, bouncy self. In her early thirties, she was not yet married. But she was madly in love with Oscar Perez, and he was in love with her. Naomi thought there'd be a big wedding before Christmas. That suspicion was confirmed when Hortencia held out her hand over the counter to Naomi. She wore a beautiful engagement ring.

"Hortencia!" Naomi screamed. "It's awesome!"

"I've found my soul mate, and he was worth waiting for!" Hortencia giggled as Naomi hugged her.

After chatting about Hortencia's plans, Naomi started to tell Hortencia about her father's birthday party. "I want it to be really special. Can Oscar play the traditional Mexican ballads? And can we have *tamales* and *enchiladas* . . . *quesadillas*, refried beans—all of Dad's favorites?"

"How many will come?" Hortencia asked.

"Oh, I think maybe fifty to sixty," Naomi said.

"That'll be fine!" Hortencia beamed, before turning serious. "Your father comes here often for *tamales*, but he usually gives me a dig. He's not too happy with us Sandovals. You probably know that."

"Yeah," Naomi nodded. "He resents Ernie and me working for Emilio Ibarra. Dad wanted his cousin to stay on the city council."

Hortencia laughed and explained, "Boy, did your daddy give me grief about the big fund-raiser we had here for Ibarra. He goes, 'Hortencia, it's a good thing you make the best *tamales* on the planet. Otherwise, I'd never darken your door again after you done that.' "

"Dad's feeling really down about turning fifty," Naomi remarked. "And he's said he doesn't want any gifts or anything special. He says he just wants to have a few beers with his buddies. But I know he'd be crushed if nobody did anything."

"What kind of gifts do you get a guy like that?" Hortencia wondered.

"Oh, Mom and me figured that out," Naomi responded. "He loves football, and we're getting him a big, flat-screen TV. He's gonna feel like those football games are right in the room with him. He'll like that. He blows off a lot of steam during the games."

They picked a date and talked a little about arrangements. Then Naomi started for home.

As Naomi walked from Hortencia's, she wondered whether she should invite the Aguirres. Her father thought highly of Clay. Dad often said what wonderful people the Aguirres were to have raised such a great son. Naomi didn't want ever to talk to Clay again. But she thought her father would be hurt if she didn't ask Clay's parents to the party.

The next day at school, Naomi spotted Clay walking alone, and she approached him. "Clay," she announced, "we're giving my dad a surprise birthday party. It's going to be two weeks from this coming Friday. Would you ask your parents if they'd like to come? You could come too, of course, with them. The party's mainly for adults, but teenagers can come with their parents. I know my dad likes you. And, well, I think he'd like to see your mom and dad."

"Hey, thanks for thinking of us," Clay responded with a big smile. Naomi hoped that he wasn't taking this invitation as a foot in the door with her. She didn't want to make such a false impression.

Naomi could tell that Clay wanted to talk more, but she hurried away. She had done her duty.

Naomi had already told Ernesto Sandoval about the party. He planned to come with his parents. *Abuela* Lena would watch the younger Sandovals at home. Abel Ruiz's parents were coming with Abel. He was going to make a special surprise dessert. Naomi would have loved to invite Carmen Ibarra and her family. But that, of course, was out of the question. Councilman Emilio Ibarra now sat in cousin Monte's seat. He was not welcome anywhere near Felix Martinez, nor was his family.

As she extended the invitations, Naomi got more and more excited about the party. But, as Dad's birthday grew nearer, he just got grumpier. After he came home from work every night, he crashed in front of the TV. When the news anchors reported on things he didn't agree with, he seemed to cuss more than usual. When he wasn't doing that, he was lamenting his meaningless life.

Before she reported for work, Naomi called Orlando with her plan. She was so nervous her stomach hurt, but it was now or never. Orlando held the key to the success of this party. It could be a life-changing time for the Martinez family—or just another party.

"Orlando," Naomi said, "we're having Dad's birthday party two weeks from Friday at Hortencia's."

"Okay," Orlando responded cautiously.

"Can you and Manny come?" Naomi asked, holding her breath. "Hortencia has already asked Oscar Perez, and he's coming. So I know you don't have a gig."

"Uh . . . yeah . . . we could come. But, *mi hermana*, do you know what you're doing?" Orlando asked.

"No," Naomi admitted, "I'm flying blind."

"So," he asked, "we should just show up? There's old Dad munching on his *enchilada*. He looks up and sees his two rotten sons on the stage?"

"Orlando," she explained, "the other day I played your song from the Perez album for Dad. He thought it was beautiful. He didn't know it was you singing, of course. But he got all mushy. He said it reminded him of the Mexican folk songs he loved as a kid. All Dad has to do is see you up there singing some wonderful traditional folk song. And I know Manny can strum a guitar. He could back you up just for the party. Dad'll be just blown away. Then, at the end of the set, you guys can come down to where Dad is sitting and . . . and . . . *you apologize*, Orlando."

"*Say what?*" Orlando gasped.

"Orlando, it's been three years!" Naomi pleaded. "I know what you did that night was to protect Mom. But if you could find it in your heart to just tell him you're sorry. And then you could wish him a happy birthday."

"Girl, I *told* you I'd never apologize," Orlando snapped.

"*Please* Orlando," Naomi begged. "Dad never lays a hard hand on Mom anymore. He hasn't done that in three years. He knows it's wrong, and he hasn't done it. He's still rude to Mom sometimes. I won't ever deny that. But he's better than he used to be."

Naomi's voice got harder. "Orlando, you could heal our family before it's too late. What if something were to happen to Dad while all this bitterness is still in our hearts. You'd never forgive yourself. You know what I'm saying is true. You'd spend the rest of your life knowing he died your enemy. He's your father, Orlando. He was good to you for a long time. You can't deny all the good times our family had. He loves you and Manny. He loves Mom too. He's just a very difficult person. But he's still our father."

"So," Orlando responded, "you want me to get on my knees and beg his forgiveness for doing the right thing that night?"

"No, Orlando," Naomi said. "Just finish your nice folk song and come down to his table. Just say, 'Dad, I'm sorry about what happened' and offer your hand. That's all. I'm not asking you for more than six words. Is that too much to ask? I mean, you *are* sorry about what happened, aren't you? We all are. I'm asking you just to be the bigger man."

Orlando was silent at the other end. Naomi could hear her brother's rapid, angry

143

breathing. Then finally he said in a voice that was barely audible, "Oh . . . okay . . . okay."

"Oh Orlando, thank you!" Naomi cried. "I love you so much. I know it'll be good. You can't imagine what it would mean to Mom if we could be a family again. Me and Mom could see you guys again any time we wanted. We wouldn't have to sneak to some out-of-the-way restaurant for fear Dad would find out. This party is as much for Mom as it is for Dad. And it's for Zack. He needs contact with his big brothers. He has creepy friends down at college who aren't good role models. He needs you and Manny in his life."

"And you think that's all it'll take, Naomi?" Orlando asked, in a cross voice. Then he started a tirade. "What makes you so sure he won't jump up and knock the table over? What makes you think he won't start cursing me and Manny for showing our faces? What makes you think he won't call me names in Spanish—every bad name he can think of?"

He was quiet for a second but soon resumed his rant. "What if he says he won't accept my apology? Maybe he'll say I'm not sincere enough. Maybe he'll tell me where to go. What makes you think he won't turn the whole party into a nightmare? He might embarrass everybody. Then things'll only be worse between us. You sure that won't happen, Naomi?"

"No," Naomi admitted quietly. "I'm not sure that won't happen. But I don't think it will. Orlando, I've seen him paging through our family picture albums. He keeps looking at us all as kids, when you were like twelve or something. You should see the look in his eyes when he does that. He looks so sad and alone. I think that deep inside he's aching to have you guys back. I think he'll grab the chance to heal our family. I pray that's what happens."

"Yeah, pray hard, girl," Orlando advised. "Because I think it's more likely that he'll go nuts and send the *enchiladas* flying."

145

"But you'll come with Manny that night and do what you promised, won't you, Orlando?" Naomi confirmed.

"Yeah," Orlando replied wearily. She'd worn her brother down. "Only for you, Naomi. I'm doing it for you—and for Mom. I believe it's a big mistake. I think it will be a disaster. But for you, I'll give it a shot."

"You've got to pick a very good traditional folk song, Orlando," Naomi instructed him. "Like the one you did on the album. A tear jerker. One that lets your beautiful voice just caress the lyrics and soar with the melody. Just like you did on the album. You know what they say. Music has charms to soothe the savage breast."

"Whoever wrote that didn't know Felix Martinez," Orlando protested.

"I love you a lot, Orlando," Naomi bubbled. "Give Manny my love too. You know, someday I'm gonna get married. I want you guys in my wedding party. I want my dad there too. I think about that,

Orlando. It'll be the happiest day of my life. And I want to share my happiness with everybody I love."

"I know," Orlando admitted. "We'll give it our best shot."

He laughed then. His was not a happy laugh. It was a rueful, wry laugh. "Wish us all luck, girl!"

CHAPTER EIGHT

At school the next day, Clay Aguirre was waiting for Naomi. He didn't look happy. "Hey Naomi," he explained, "my parents, they said to thank you for the invite. But they got stuff going on. They just can't make it. They're closing deals and things like that."

Naomi looked at Clay. She had met his parents often when she and Clay were dating. They were always polite to Naomi. But she got the distinct feeling that they looked down on the Martinez family. They owned a nicer home than her parents did. It was a newer, more modern home on a larger lot. Most of the houses on the streets named for birds were old, small, stucco, one-story houses on small lots. Naomi's dad was a construction worker; Mr. Aguirre was a college-educated financial advisor.

"That's okay, Clay," Naomi replied. "There'll still be a lot of people there."

Ernesto Sandoval came along then. He gave Clay a dirty look, and Clay took off. Ernesto waited until Clay was gone before talking with Naomi. "Hey, Naomi, me and Dad found the perfect birthday gift for your dad. I know he's a big Charger fan. But I know he was rooting for the New Orleans Saints at the Super Bowl. So we went on eBay and got him a cool Saints jersey and cap."

"Oh Ernie, that's perfect," Naomi said.

"How's it going with Orlando and Manny?" Ernesto asked. "Did you pull it off?"

"Yeah," Naomi groaned. "And it wasn't easy. Orlando is sure it'll be a big disaster. He's afraid that Dad will freak and ruin everything. Orlando thinks the minute Dad sees him and Manny, he'll be furious. What

149

do you think, Ernie? Am I being a complete fool?"

Ernesto put his arm around Naomi and gave her a squeeze. "Babe," he assured her, "it'll work. I know your dad pretty well. He's a rough character. But deep down there's a heart, a big heart. I'm betting on that."

"Thanks for saying that, Ernie," Naomi said. "I needed you to say that even if you don't believe it."

"I *do* believe it, babe," Ernesto insisted.

"Ernie," Naomi told him, "Abel texted me. He's making flan for the party. He makes this special chocolate *flan*. It is just heavenly. He's so sweet."

"Yeah, he's my best friend," Ernesto agreed. "Abel's dad, Sal, he gets along good with your dad. They're both hardworking guys, no pretenses."

"You know, Ernie," Naomi commented, "I invited some of the guys who work with Dad. I was so surprised how much they like my father. They're really excited about the party. Eppy said my dad always has his back, especially when something goes wrong on the job. Eppy told me dad saved his job once. Dad covered for one of Eppy's mistakes."

"Naomi," Ernesto asked, "how are you going to work this? How are you getting your dad down to Hortencia's that night?"

"Oh, I told him me and Mom and Zack just want a little family get-together at Hortencia's for his birthday," she explained. "I told him we wanted to take him out for some of those *tamales* he likes so much. No big deal. I don't think he liked the idea, but he went along with it."

Naomi had just one more river to cross: Monte Esposito. Dad still thought the world of him. Dad believed the whole indictment was a raw deal, a lynching of a good man. Naomi and almost everybody else didn't think so. But excluding Monte from the party would be a huge slap in the face to Dad.

Ernesto drove Naomi over to the beautiful two-story home where the Espositos lived. The house was large. Naomi thought the Martinez, Sandoval, and Ruiz houses would all fit inside it with room to spare.

Naomi expected to find Monte, who had posted bail, to be in a down mood. But he was as happy and as outgoing as usual. Naomi introduced Ernesto as her boyfriend. Luckily, Monte didn't know he and Naomi had both worked for Emilio Zapata Ibarra.

"Come on in," Monte invited them, leading them into a huge living room filled with elegant furniture. Naomi thought probably some of the pieces were gifts from people whom he helped in an illegal way. On one wall hung a huge color photograph of Monte Esposito and his wife with the president of the United States.

Naomi wasn't going to ask Monte how his legal troubles were going. But he brought the subject up. "My lawyers are getting those little problems taken care of," he declared. "Everything's on schedule. It's nothing more than a few ants at a picnic!" Monte laughed.

"That's good," Naomi replied, not sure whether she believed him. "*Tío* Monte, you know my dad is turning fifty. We're having a party for him at Hortencia's. I hope you and *mi tía* can come. It would mean a lot to Dad."

"Wouldn't miss it for the world," Monte boomed. "My cousin, Felix, he's a great guy. The salt of the earth."

A maid brought coffee and elegant little cakes. They sat for a while, sipping coffee and catching up on family matters. Monte Esposito lived in a whole other world from what Naomi had always known. The man leaned back in a leather chair and posed a question. "Know what I miss most about not being on the city council? I can't bring a little glamour into the lives of the little people—like your dad, Naomi."

Ernesto glanced quickly at Naomi. Monte Esposito didn't notice. He was too busy with what he was saying. "They lead lives of hard work and drudgery. I was able to get your dad into some nice parties. Your

153

poor dad, he's got a dirty little job, a lousy life. He works like a dog. But occasionally he got to go to glitzy events and feel like a big shot. That meant a lot to me, to give him that."

Naomi resented that take on her father's life. Dad didn't have a "dirty little job." He had an important skilled job that made tall buildings rise. He was very good at what he did, and he made great money. Naomi didn't agree with Monte Esposito. Felix Martinez's life was just fine, even without invitations to stupid galas from his crooked cousin. But Naomi didn't want any trouble. So she said nothing to argue with the man. But Naomi did say, "Dad's a really skilled crane operator. He can manipulate that crane better than anybody. He's proud of that."

Monte laughed. "Poor guy, trying to see some meaning in his life. Well, good for him. And good that you're giving him this party, Naomi. Keep his spirits up. I'll be there with bells on to swell the crowd.

Can't be too many people coming. But we'll make up for lack of quantity with quality, eh?" He laughed again.

As Naomi and Ernesto were going down the driveway to the Volvo, Ernesto had to make a comment. "What a pompous jerk! He's been indicted by the grand jury as a bribe-taking crook. And he's looking down on your skilled, hardworking, honest father. What an idiot!"

"Dad has always idolized him," Naomi responded, shaking her head. "It makes me sick. I didn't even want to invite him, but I had no choice."

During the drive back to the *barrio*, they had reached Washington Street. On that street, they passed the bar and grill that Esposito allegedly got a license for in exchange for a bribe. "Look at that joint," Ernesto remarked bitterly. "Two drunks staggering out now. They're probably looking for their car so they can kill somebody on their way home."

"Ernie!" Naomi cried. "That's Zack and the creep he knows from college, Steve somebody."

"But even idiots like the Saenz brothers got to know you don't serve liquor to a seventeen-year-old," Ernesto commented.

"Probably Steve bought a bottle and shared it with Zack in the bathroom," Naomi explained. "Steve's twenty-two. I hate for Zack to hang with somebody like him."

Ernesto slowed to a stop, and they watched the pair cross the street. "Oh man, Ernie!" Naomi pointed. "There's Dad's pickup. Zack must have borrowed it. Don't tell me one of them is going to try to drive!"

"Well, it ain't happenin'," Ernesto declared with sudden determination. He pulled the Volvo alongside the pickup. Ernesto stepped from the car and hailed Naomi's brother. "Hey Zack, what's goin' down?"

Usually Zack was shy and soft-spoken, but now he was buzzed. He grinned at

Ernesto as he replied. "My buddy Steve had a little too much to drink. So I'm driving us home." Zack was unsteady on his feet, and he had trouble inserting the key in the car door lock.

"Zack, buddy," Ernesto said in a friendly voice, "I think you had a little too much to drink too. Tell you what. I'll drive Steve home in my Volvo, and Naomi can drive the pickup home. Okay?"

"Come on, dude," Zack whined indignantly. The liquor had changed his personality dramatically. Just like his father, Zack became a different person when he drank. "I'm not drunk. I'm perfectly capable of driving my friend Steve home. So kindly get out of my way."

Steve was propped on one arm against the truck. And he was getting angry. "Who's this dude sticking his nose in here?" he demanded.

"I'm almost eighteen years old," Zack told Ernesto. "And I don't need you to stick your nose in where it's not wanted, Ernie.

Me and Steve are going home now, and I'm driving."

Steve glared at Ernesto and commanded, "Get lost, man." He looked like a mean drunk.

"In two minutes I'm calling the cops," Ernesto threatened. "I'm not letting you drive drunk, Zack. No way is that gonna happen, even if I have to deck you dude."

"Oh man, I'm outta here!" Steve yelled, turning sharply. He staggered down the street toward the bus stop.

"Look what you did!" Zack yelled. "You embarrassed me in fronta my friend!"

"You want a DUI, Zack?" Ernesto barked in his face. "You want to lose your driver's license for a whole year? That's the least of it. Maybe going home drunk you'll kill a kid on a bike. Then you're looking at half a dozen years in the slammer. You really want that, Zack?"

"I'm driving the pickup home," Zack snarled. "Get out of my way, Ernie!" He stabbed the keys into the door and swung it open. He was starting to get in when Ernesto grabbed him and yanked him out.

"No way, dude," Ernesto insisted, pushing Zack against the door of the pickup. "I might have to hog-tie you and throw you into the bed of the pickup. But you're not taking the wheel. Three teenagers just been killed this year driving drunk. You want to do this to your father? He thinks you're the best thing since sliced bread man."

"You want my father to see me being brought home like a baby by you, Sandoval? Who do you think you are?" Zack protested in a shaky voice. "I drove the pickup from our house, and I'm taking it home."

Ernesto grabbed the boy's shoulders and gave him a shake. "So help me, Zack, I'm whipping your behind if you don't lissen to reason," Ernesto yelled in the boy's face.

"I hate you, Sandoval," Zack snarled. "You're a big jerk. You think you're better

159

than anybody else. My sister must be crazy to hang out with you!"

Naomi hopped into the cab of the pickup. Ernesto walked Zack around to the passenger side and got him into the cab too. Ernesto returned to the Volvo and followed the pickup to the house on Bluebird Street. Both vehicles pulled into the driveway of the Martinez household.

Felix Martinez was in the front yard playing with Brutus as the two vehicles arrived. The only thing that seemed to put him in a good mood lately was playing with his pit bull.

"Hey, what's this now?" Mr. Martinez demanded. "Zack took the pickup a coupla hours ago. What are you doin' at the wheel, Naomi. What's goin' on here?" He turned and glared at Ernesto, who was getting out of the Volvo. "What's he doin' here? What the devil is this? Zack, you said you and Steve were goin' for hamburgers. Where's Steve?"

Zack got out of the pickup and almost fell on his face. Felix Martinez rushed forward and steadied his son against the fender. "Zack, I'm not believing my own eyes, boy. What's wrong with you? You're drunk! You're drunk as a skunk!" the man bellowed.

"It's not my fault, Dad," Zack whimpered. The sight of his angry father sobered him a little. "Me and Steve were doin' fine. We come out of the . . . the place . . . and we were goin' home. I was gonna drive Steve and then come home here. Steve, he'd been drinkin', see? And I didn't think he ought to be drivin'. So I was gonna take him home and then . . . ."

Naomi finished the explanation for her brother. "Dad, Steve decided to take the bus when Ernesto wouldn't let either of them drive the pickup." She was speaking in a calm voice. "We were driving down Washington, me and Ernie. And we saw your pickup, Dad. Well, Steve and Zack were heading toward it . . . ."

Zack looked at his father, searching the man's face for some sign of understanding. Terror was sobering Zack fast. "Dad, you always said somebody's got to be the designated driver when someone gets buzzed. I wouldn't let Steve drive, 'cause he had a lot more to drink than me. I did what you told me, Dad."

"*I* told you to go drinkin' with that lowlife Steve?" Mr. Martinez demanded. "Having a coupla beers at home is one thing. Getting loaded at a bar and driving home is a whole 'nother. Who served booze to a kid like you, Zack?"

"Steve just gave me a sip from his bottle," Zack explained. "Just a sip, Dad. I was okay to drive. Ernie come and hassled us, me and Steve. He's a big jerk. It was him caused the trouble."

Felix Martinez grabbed Zack's shirtfront and pushed his face close to his son's. "Get in the house, fool! I've lost my two older boys, and you're all I got left. Now you get wasted and try to drive my truck! Get outta my sight!"

Ernesto thought it best to say nothing. He thought Naomi would be more successful doing the talking.

"Dad," Naomi said, "we were so scared that Zack would get in an accident or something. We had to stop him from driving. I couldn't have done it, but Ernie was able to."

Felix Martinez cast a glance at Ernesto. "A man works his backside off for thirty years. What has he got to show for it? Two sons who hate him. They don't even want to see his face no more. And a little punk— only seventeen years old—who gets drunk and tries to drive like that. I'd like to go in that house and whip that little punk to a pulp," he threatened darkly.

"Mr. Martinez," Ernesto finally said, "Zack's a really good kid. We all make mistakes. It was just a mistake. I don't think he'll ever do something like that again. Take it easy, Mr. Martinez. You got a good kid there. He idolizes you. Cut him some slack."

Felix Martinez stared hard at Ernesto. The boy might have been an alien getting out of a UFO that just landed on the lawn.

"Listen to him!" Mr. Martinez exclaimed, shaking his head and speaking to no one in particular. He couldn't believe what had just happened. "This sixteen-year-old kid is tellin' a fifty-year-old father how to deal with his kid. This little sixteen-year-old punk is spouting wisdom to a guy old enough to be his grandfather."

Felix Martinez was beside himself. He turned around toward the door. His hands were stretched out from his body, palms up. "This," he went on, with a jerk of his head, "is the Sandovals for you."

The man strode off toward the house, complaining to the world at large. "You gotta hand it to that wimpy Luis Sandoval. You gotta give it up for that prissy school teacher in his little red tie and his shiny suit. He raised a kid like this. You gotta hand it to that twit Luis Sandoval." He disappeared inside the house.

Naomi glanced at Ernesto and then hurried into the house after her father.

CHAPTER NINE

Inside the house, Naomi tensed. She remembered the first time Orlando got drunk and came home driving like that. He knocked over the family mailbox. Orlando was about the same age Zack was now— seventeen. Dad's yelling could be heard all over the neighborhood. But Orlando wasn't Zack. When his father screamed at him, Orlando gave it back in kind. Naomi remembered the bitter fight. She was thirteen years old, and she remembered Orlando yelling, "Who are you to talk, Dad? How many times you stopped at the bar on the way home from work? You come home drunk!" He threw Dad's scolding right back into his father's face. That was Orlando.

Now Naomi prepared for the worst. Dad was going to go after Zack. She feared he would express his rage and frustration just as he did with Orlando. Now, not only was Dad shocked that Zack would do such a thing. He had been humiliated when Ernesto Sandoval had to get his kid home.

"What's the matter with you?" Dad yelled at Zack. "I thought you had more sense, boy. You know what coulda happened? You coulda got into an accident and maybe hurt or killed somebody? You know what a DUI woulda cost us? What do you think I'm feeling like right now? I'd like to take you by the scruff of your neck and shake you like the cat shakes a mouse. That's what I'd like to do. Ain't I been through enough with your brothers who disappeared on me?"

"I'm sorry, Dad," Zack almost wept. "I'm sorry. I didn't want to drink. Steve got a bottle and said I should drink a little. I didn't want to, but Steve said I was a wimp. I was ashamed. So I drank from the bottle."

"That Steve is a dirtbag," Dad declared. "Don't you be hanging with him no more."

"I won't, Dad," Zack obeyed contritely. "You're right. He's no good." Zack was almost completely sober now, shocked by what almost happened. It was so unlike him to do something like that.

"All right then," Felix Martinez said, the anger draining from him. "Lissen up, boy. You mean everything to me, you hear me? Guy down at the job, he had a boy your age. Last year, the kid got to driving drunk and wrapped his car around a tree. He was dead at the scene. Nate had to go down to the hospital and identify his dead boy. Nate's a tough guy, but he cried like a baby. I can't take something like that, y'hear me? You're the only son I got left, Zack. Orlando and Manny, they don't exist for me no more. They don't care if I'm dead or alive."

"Orlando and Manny care about you too, Dad," Zack told him.

Naomi froze. "Oh no," she thought, "Zack's going to break his promise and tell

Dad about the birthday party. He's going to ruin everything."

"Nah, they don't even want to see me," Dad protested. "They won't even come to my funeral when it happens. You'll see. When they put me in the ground, those bums won't even be coming around."

"You're not gonna die for a long time, Dad," Zack responded. "You're strong. You better not die, Dad. You're a great Dad, and I need you."

Naomi didn't see Dad hugging Zack. She was already in her room, but she knew that's what he was doing. She breathed a long sigh of relief. Zack had remembered his promise.

When Naomi saw Ernesto the next day at school, she told him what had happened at home. "That was so good what you told my dad about Zack being a good guy, Ernie," she told him. "It really sunk in. He handled it real well because of that. He'd never admit you influenced him, but you did."

Ernesto smiled. "Good. I was afraid I'd given your father another reason to hate me."

"For a minute," Naomi told Ernesto, "while Zack was talking to Dad, I thought he was going to blow the surprise. But thank heaven he didn't. I almost ran into the living room and clamped my hand over his mouth!"

Naomi giggled nervously. "Mom's getting so excited about the party, but she's terrified too. She's afraid Dad will run out of Hortencia's the minute he sees his sons. She's worried they'll never get the chance to talk to him. Mom always expects the worst. Not that I'm not scared too, 'cause I am."

At lunchtime, Naomi called Orlando again on her cell. "Everything still cool, Orlando?" she asked.

"We're still coming," he replied. "I don't know how cool things'll be, but we're coming."

Naomi told Orlando what happened with Zack. "Poor Zack, he just crumbled into a pitiful heap when Dad tongue-lashed him. Remember the time you came home wasted, Orlando. Dad yelled at you and—"

"I gave back as good as I got, yeah," Orlando answered proudly. "He never could browbeat me, Naomi. I think that's why he got so mad at me. But that drunk-driving incident was not my finest moment."

"You're still going to say you're sorry, aren't you Orlando?" Naomi asked.

"Don't remind me," her brother responded. "I promised I would and I will. The words are going to stick in my throat, but I'll spit them out somehow. But if he starts yelling and trying to take me down, I'm not just standing there. If he won't accept what I have to say, then I'm done. I'm not Zack. I won't grovel. You understand that, don't you, Naomi?"

"Yeah, I know," Naomi agreed. "I don't expect you to grovel, Orlando. Just say you're sorry, and we'll hope for the best."

"You got my word," Orlando assured her.

Linda Martinez was going to great pains all week to make her husband's favorite meals. She always tried to please him by making what he liked, but this week she was going overboard. Mom, Zack, and Naomi all liked vegetables like broccoli and squash. But none of that appeared the week before Dad's birthday.

"Hey!" Felix Martinez said on Monday. "This here is pretty good lasagna, Linda. It's got different cheeses—parmesan, mozzarella. How come you don't always make it like this? This is pretty darn good."

"Thank you, Felix," Mom glowed. "I'll try to remember to always make it like this."

Then, on Tuesday, Naomi's mother made Mexican pizza.

"This stuff is all right," her husband declared. "If you'd cook more like this all the time, I wouldn't always be goin' for takeout food. You know, you're gettin' to be a pretty good cook in your old age."

"Mom's not old," Naomi protested, "and neither are you, Dad. I just saw on TV that a seventy-eight-year-old man is climbing Mount Everest. He's almost to the top. He doesn't think he's old. He's having fun."

"No, the guy is crazy," Dad said. "The old dude has lost his marbles, or he wouldn't be clawing his way up a mountain at his age. Matter of fact, all these guys climbing mountains are nuts. What's the good in it?"

Felix Martinez glanced across the table at his wife and children. "Now, on Friday night, we're all goin' over to Hortencia's, right? No big deal. Just the family, just the four of us. We'll get there about seven, eat some of her nice *tamales*, and then we come home. Right? I don't like Hortencia because she worked for Ibarra. But other than that she's okay. She's a lot of fun, always friendly and smiling."

A big bite of Mexican pizza disappeared into Dad's mouth. "Humph," he mumbled. "Good. . . . Anyway, the guys I work with, Eppy and Pogo and Roto and them, they want to hang with me on my birthday. So I'll get together with them later on, have some beers. We're all pretty close. We'll drink and talk about the good old days when our whole lives were before us instead of behind us."

Felix Martinez got a philosophical look on his face, as he munched his pizza. "Those guys, they're kinda more family to me than some of my own family. They'd give me the shirts off their backs, and I'd do the same for them. They like me. They wanna be with me. Not like those lousy bums I got for sons, Orlando and Manny. Here it is, my birthday coming up, the big five-oh. And I haven't even gotten a card from those lousy bums."

Naomi concentrated on the pizza. Zack looked nervous, as if somehow Dad would find out about the big conspiracy. "Well," Mom declared, "it will be nice at Hortencia's." She kept a straight, impassive face. Naomi was proud of her.

Friday night would be their healing, Naomi thought. Or it would be the last glimmer of hope blinking out.

Naomi couldn't bear the thought that the party might be a failure. She worried about its failing. She prayed for success. She went to Our Lady of Guadalupe Church, as her mother did. She lit a whole row of candles for her special intention—the healing of her family. She prayed before the picture of Our Lady right above the candles, the virgin who looked like an Indian girl.

Meanwhile, Dad kept on talking. "Yeah," he was saying. "Me and Eppy go back the longest. We were just dumb kids when we started in the construction business. Eppy lugged sacks of mortar, and I wasn't much better off. I got more training, though. I was always getting new skills. I went up to being good with the big machines. Eppy, he was afraid to do that. He's still on the lower rungs of the ladder."

Dad paused long enough to chew and swallow more pizza. "But you know what?" he continued, "Eppy has a great family. Go figure. He ain't been able to do for his kids like I done for mine. But you should see his sons. They're macho boys, but they come right up to their father and kiss him. Right there in front of everybody. They ain't ashamed to show their love. They respect the man. Wish I could have sons like that instead of Orlando and Manny. I'd give up my job on the crane and the money too. Lissen, I'd give up in a minute. I'd do a dirty menial job like Eppy if I had boys like him who . . . loved him."

"I love you, Daddy," Naomi told him.

"Me too," Zack added. "I love you too, Dad."

"You're okay, you two," Dad assured them. "But once I had four kids. Yep. There were four kids, and now there's just two. I'm battin' five hundred, and that's okay in baseball. But not when you're talking about your own flesh and blood. You can't help having feelings, even for the half that's gone. It rips up a man's soul."

Dad finished the Mexican pizza and declared, "To have half your family gone bad, that ain't easy."

"Orlando and Manny aren't bad," Linda Martinez insisted. "They're just foolish and stubborn."

"Orlando is bad to the bone, Linda, and Manny follows him," Dad stated. "Orlando raised his hand against his own father. It don't get any worse than that. He ain't never said he was sorry. In all these years, wouldn't you think he'd of come around and said he was sorry? No, he's a no good bum. Manny too. Manny wanted to hang out on the streets and get into all kinds of trouble. I had to throw the both of them out. I thought maybe they'd come to their senses. Maybe they'd come home, but . . ." Dad's voice trailed off. He sat silently, shaking his head.

They were all silent around the table. Naomi and Zack glanced at each other.

Mom looked tense. Naomi could see the dread in her mother's eyes, the terrible fear that it would all go wrong.

"Remember, Dad," Naomi asked, "when we used to take vacations in the summer? We haven't done that in a long time. Remember when we went to the Grand Canyon and rode all around the rim? That was so cool. We should go someplace this summer."

"Yeah," Dad recalled. "But all that stuff was before Orlando and Manny went bad. It wouldn't be the same now."

"I've always wanted to go to Yellowstone," Naomi said. "We've never been there. I'd like to see Old Faithful. They say Yellowstone is the most beautiful of the national parks. We could rent a motor home and go this summer."

Felix Martinez sighed.

"We don't even tailgate anymore at the Charger games," Naomi went on.

"Yeah, well," Dad shrugged. "You guys got older. You didn't want to be doing stupid stuff with the old man anymore. You wanted to be with your friends. Naomi, you wanted to be hanging out with Ernie. Zack, pretty soon you'll get a chick. You won't be around here much either."

"I don't have a girlfriend," Zack said. "I'd like to tailgate again when the Chargers start doing good. We could barbecue *carne asada*."

"Yeah," Naomi added. "Ernie would even come along. He said his family never did that, and it sounds like fun."

"Ernie, he's kind of a wimp," Dad commented. "I'm surprised he even likes football."

"Yeah, he loves football," Naomi replied. "You shoulda seen how excited he got watching the homecoming game."

"You know," Dad said, "we should be finished at Hortencia's about eight maybe, right? Then me and the guys can go to the bar. Maybe a couple other guys will come. Eppy acted a little funny when I talked to him about it. I wouldn't be surprised if

Eppy and them had a kind of surprise. I told them not to do anything. I don't want no big deal. I think I'll call Eppy now. We oughta tell Harry down at the bar that half a dozen of us'll be comin' in. I like getting' our usual place near the TV."

Naomi, Zack, and their mother exchanged looks.

Dad got on his cell phone. "Hey Eppy, how's it goin'?" The two friends exchanged greetings. Then Dad got to the point of the call.

"You know, Eppy, I figure I'll get to the bar around eight. I oughta be done with the family thing at Hortencia's by then. Do you want to call Harry and let him know when the guys are comin'? We'd like that table near the TV."

For a few minutes Dad just listened, and then he looked perplexed. When he closed the phone, he said, "Eppy, he's acting weird. He's acting like he ain't even interested in going to the bar Friday for my birthday. Even Eppy don't want to help me celebrate my lousy fiftieth birthday." Dad's laugh was a mixture of sadness and bitterness. "Maybe I thought Eppy was a better friend than he is. I mean, why should he be wanting to hang out with me when he's got this great family?"

Felix Martinez turned to his wife. His eyes were underscored with sorrow. "We gotta be prepared for how it's gonna be around here pretty soon, Linda. There'll just be the two of us sittin' here lookin' at each other. Two of our kids already gone from our lives. Pretty soon we'll be losing the other two. It'll just be the two of us, starin' at each other and wonderin' where the years went." Dad smiled an unconvincing smile. He was trying to be flip. "We might not even remember we ever had kids. We'll have to check out the pictures in the albums. We'll be wondering who those people are who looked so happy . . . a long time ago."

CHAPTER TEN

Right after school let out on Friday, Naomi met Ernesto and Abel at Hortencia's. All the colorful decorations were in place, as well as the pottery, the masks, and the painted cutouts. Ernesto brought the balloons and streamers.

"Oh Hortencia!" Naomi cried in delight. She was looking at the huge printed banner that read "*Feliz cumpleaños*, Felix Martinez." Naomi threw her arms around Hortencia for a big hug. "You're the best!" she squealed.

"Well, we must bring a smile to that man's face," Hortencia declared with a giggle. "When he comes in here for his *tamales*, he's always so grumpy. He is so mad at the world. It got really bad when his cousin lost the city council seat. I hope this party will show him how much he is loved by his family and friends.

"Yeah," Naomi agreed, "the guys from work are coming. So are some of his cronies from the neighborhood. Eppy's his best friend. Dad was planning to meet him and the other guys down at the bar after we finish here. He's thinking we'll just gobble down our *tamales* and leave. Poor Eppy knows about the party here 'cause he's coming. So he was acting a little weird. Now Dad thinks even Eppy doesn't like him!"

Hortencia turned serious. She knew the sad story of the Martinez sons. Orlando and Manny had been missing from the family circle for years now. Hortencia also knew the boys were coming tonight with the Oscar Perez band. They would be performing for the party. She knew tonight's party was part of the big effort to reconcile everybody. "Oscar called me and said the bus would be coming in at six. Everything is on schedule," Hortencia reported. "Oscar knows all about what's going on. He's really close to Orlando and Manny. Oscar is only thirty-five, but he's very wise. He's been telling the boys to make this reconciliation work tonight. Oscar told them that nobody loves you like your parents. You don't throw that relationship away."

"I don't worry so much about Manny," Naomi remarked. "But Orlando is too much like Dad. He's hotheaded and stubborn. I'm afraid. What if Dad doesn't respond well to his first words? Will Orlando just turn on his heel and stomp off cussing. That just terrifies me."

Hortencia gave Naomi a comforting hug. "The guys aren't wearing their regular out-fits," she told Naomi. "They're playing it real loose. T-shirts, jeans, ball caps. Just them and their guitars. Orlando has been rehearsing with his brother for the last hour or so."

"Perfect!" Naomi replied cheerfully. In her mind, she wondered whether her brothers were just being ready to make a fast getaway if things went wrong.

Naomi looked around. Ernesto was on a ladder, hanging the last of the balloons and sparkling streamers. In all the time he had been with Naomi, the breach between her father and his sons overshadowed their happiness together. The break was never completely off Naomi's mind. Ernesto desperately wanted it to end tonight. He knew it would be touch-and-go. He couldn't get involved. The family had to do it on their own.

"There's the table where your family will sit, Naomi," Hortencia pointed. "It has the best view of the stage. The candles will be lit, and dinner will be served before the Oscar Perez band appears. Then, right before Abel and the servers bring the dessert—Abel's chocolate flan—Oscar and the band will come on stage. I told Oscar that Orlando and Manny must stay out of sight for the first number. Then, with the spotlight on them, Orlando and Manny will appear. Orlando will sing this special ballad from Veracruz that he's been rehearsing. He'll accompany himself on the guitar, and Manny will strum along too. That's the moment when the magic will begin to happen . . ."

Naomi picked things up from there. "Orlando and Manny will come off stage and walk directly over to Dad. Orlando promised to extend his hand and say he's sorry for what happened. He promised to do that." There was a catch in Naomi's throat. She was growing more nervous by the minute. The party was still four hours away, and already her legs felt like cooked noodles.

Ernesto saw how scared Naomi was. He walked over and put his arm around her. "It'll be great, babe."

A nightmare scenario kept playing out in Naomi's mind. Orlando holds out his hand. He says he's sorry, but in a kind of blunt way. He won't say it as Zack would, in a genuine, contrite way. Dad will sense

Orlando's lack of feeling. Dad will refuse to take his son's hand. Instead, he'll jump up from the table, maybe knocking it over. He'll yell at everybody that it was wrong to trick him like this. He'll explode at Naomi, Mom, even Zack.

Naomi could hear Dad's furious voice. "How could you deceive me like this? My own family! How could you humiliate me like this? Look at Orlando, look at the bum! He's not sorry! He's sneering at me right now! You betrayed me, all of you, and in front of everybody. In front of my friends, in front of Eppy and Roto and Pogo. In front of that wimp Luis Sandoval and his family. In front of the Ruiz family. I am humiliated in front of the whole *barrio*!"

"Oh Ernie, I'm so scared," Naomi admitted.

Ernesto held her tighter. "It'll be fine," he said assuredly. "I can feel it. I know it."

Ernesto drove Naomi home and briefly went into the house. Felix Martinez seemed in an especially bad mood. The dreaded birthday had arrived. He was sitting in his favorite chair with a glum look on his face. He glanced at his watch and said, "An hour from now we go to Hortencia's. We eat *tamales* and pretend it's a birthday celebration. Like fifty is a reason to celebrate."

Naomi and Mom exchanged a worried look.

"It's all downhill from here," Dad declared.

"You look great, Mr. Martinez," Ernesto commented, "and you're still at the top of your game."

"Listen to the phony trying to make me feel good," Dad sneered. "All right Ernie, you gave it your best shot. You sent it up the flagpole, and it didn't fly. I just want this stupid dinner to be over. I just want me and my pals to go to the bar and get some beers. That's all I want."

He got a wistful look on his face then. "I remember when Monte turned fifty. What a party he had. Musta been fifty people at least. Everybody loves Monte. He's king of the mountain. I don't care what that lynch mob tried to do. He's still the guy."

"Well," Ernesto announced, "I better be going now. You guys have fun tonight."

"Oh yeah," Felix Martinez grunted, "the four of us chowing down *tamales* at Hortencia's. That'll be a blast all right. The four of us sittin' there. Now ain't that a deal for a man turnin' fifty?"

Ernesto went out the door after scratching Brutus behind the ears. He felt sorry again for Naomi living in this house. He didn't think he could cope with that kind of homelife. It was oppressive. How do you deal with a family member who was always bitter and angry? How do you live with someone who could find little or no reason to be thankful or to laugh. That was a darkness that never lifted. It just settled in on everybody. No matter how hard anyone tried, there would be no light. It seeped into their hearts and minds and souls until everybody was as sad as Felix Martinez.

Ernesto marveled at how Naomi was able to rise above it all. She was so much fun and loving and a joy to be with.

"Well," Linda Martinez announced at twenty minutes to seven, "I'm all dressed. You want to put on a jacket, Felix? That nice navy blue jacket looks good on you."

Naomi's father looked at his wife. "What are we getting' dressed up for?" he asked. "To go eat *tamales* at that joint? I ain't seen you in that lavender dress since Lydia's wedding. And the pearls . . . you're wearing pearls?"

"Felix, you gave me these pearls last Christmas," Mom explained in a faltering voice.

Felix Martinez sighed and put on his navy blue jacket. Naomi thought he looked very handsome. The four of them marched out to the family sedan. They used the sedan whenever all of them went out—the few times they did. Nobody looked happy. Judging by the expressions on their faces, they might have been heading for an execution.

As they drove down Tremayne Street, Felix Martinez expressed a glum hope. "I hope there ain't anybody we know there at Hortencia's. I'd hate for one of my friends to see this pathetic little bunch celebrating my lousy birthday."

When they got close to Hortencia's, Dad looked alarmed. "Hey!" he cried. "They got something else goin' on here tonight! Some big shindig goin' on. Look at all those parked cars! There ain't gonna be room for us. We better turn around and find some other joint."

"No!" Naomi said abruptly. "Those people are all on the patio. There'll be plenty of room for us inside." Her heart was pounding madly. She could scarcely breathe.

"This is crazy," Dad complained. "Look at them all goin' in. What the devil is goin' on? How come none of you geniuses called up to make sure nothin' else was goin' on tonight?"

Dad peered through the windshield. "Look, there's the Sandovals goin' in with Ernie. And there's the Ruiz gang."

Sal Ruiz broke away from his family. He came over toward Felix Martinez, who was now out of the car. "Hey man, congratulations," Sal called out. "Some kind of turnout, eh?"

"What?" Dad gasped.

Eppy and his wife, Magdalena, came by. Eppy gave Felix Martinez a bear hug, "*Feliz cumpleaños, amigo!*" he shouted.

They all surged around Mr. Martinez then—Pogo, Roto, some of the younger guys too. They were slapping him on the back. They told him how good he looked, that he had plenty of fire left in him. They were laughing and high-fiving him. Luis Sandoval shook his hand.

Then Monte Esposito came out of his BMW and shouted, "Hey Felix, you look like a million bucks, cousin. Hey, what're we celebrating here? Some big shot must be having a birthday! I never saw so many people."

Felix Martinez embraced his cousin, and they walked arm in arm into Hortencia's.

Hortencia escorted the Martinez family to their special table. The candles were already lit. The glow from them cast an eerie light on Mr. Martinez's face. He glanced at the balloons, the streamers, and the banner with his name on it. Then he looked at his family seated around him.

"You knew this was happening. You all knew," he accused them.

"Yes," Naomi spoke up. "We wanted a nice party so you'd know how much we all love you, Daddy."

Tears ran down Linda Martinez's face. She reached over and grasped her husband's hand. She whispered, "All our friends wanted to come. They wanted to be part of this because they love you too."

Hortencia served a sumptuous meal of chicken *enchiladas*, *quesadillas*, *tamales*, *carne asada,* and all the trimmings. Felix Martinez kept looking around in amazement. This was a larger party than even Monte Esposito had when he turned fifty.

Then Oscar Perez and his band minus two performers appeared. Even in their T-shirts and jeans, the band members took command of the room. Perez bid everyone *"Buenos noches!"* and the crowd applauded and greeted him back. Then he nodded to the band, and they began to play. He sang a traditional folk ballad, ending with a rousing, *"Feliz cumpleaños*, Felix!" The applause seemed to make the masks on the walls jump. Felix Martinez stared at the smiling faces of his friends, a look of near shock in his eyes.

And then the spotlight turned on two young men who had emerged on a darkened part of the stage. They carried guitars. One of the young men moved to the center of the stage. The other stood at his side, playing soft chords on his guitar.

Orlando Martinez began to sing a folk ballad from Veracruz. His sweetly soft and tender tones quickly vaulted into a powerful, emotional tenor.

Naomi thought she was going to faint. She almost dared not look at her father, but she finally forced herself to glance at him. She saw a look of total astonishment on Dad's face.

Felix Martinez stared at his sons on the stage. Orlando's voice soared into the bittersweet lyrics of the song. His father's gaze was riveted on him. Naomi stole several glances at her father. She was trying to sense what he was feeling, but he was expressionless, except for shock. His face seemed carved of stone.

When he finished his song, the audience was silent. Almost everyone in the room knew the importance of this moment. Ernesto Sandoval and his family knew, and the others did too. Orlando and Manny stepped off the stage and approached their father. Those who best knew the Martinezes felt their hearts stop, as did Naomi, her mother, and brother.

Within moments, the tall, handsome young man who looked like a younger version of Felix Martinez was standing at his father's table. Manny stood alongside him.

"Dad," Orlando said softly. "I'm sorry about what happened." His dark eyes met his father's. Orlando held out his hand. *"Feliz cumpleaños, mi padre."*

For one terrible moment that seemed to last for an eternity, *Felix Martinez did not take Orlando's hand.*

Naomi Martinez thought her heart would break into a million pieces. If it did, it would never completely come together again.

As had happened in Naomi's worst nightmare, her father got up from his chair so fast that he almost knocked it over.

Then Naomi's father reached out and embraced Orlando, kissing him on both cheeks. Then he took Manny in his arms and kissed him too.

For the first time in her life, Naomi saw her father cry—*really* cry.

Tears streamed down the tough man's face. He was shaking with emotion. Both sons kissed their father. Naomi saw tears on their cheeks as well. They hugged again, and the room broke out in loud applause, cheers, and whistles. The Sandoval and Ruiz families knew what had just happened. Others—close friends like Eppy—knew as well. They all gave a ringing, pounding applause, accompanied by wild cheers.

One of the waiters pulled up two more chairs to the Martinez table. The two sons sat to the left and right of their father. Abel Ruiz and two waiters carried in the chocolate *flan* dessert that Abel had prepared.

Felix Martinez had yet to say a word. Then the lights were turned down. In his serving of *flan*, a tiny candle flickered. Everybody yelled for him to make a wish, and it would come true. And then he finally spoke in a trembling voice.

"There's nothing more to wish for," the man announced. Looking to his left and right, he declared, "I got it all." He wrapped

an arm around either son and repeated himself in a booming voice. "*I got it all!*"

Naomi Martinez thought that, no matter
how long she lived, this memory would be
her best. It would be the most beautiful and
amazing moment of her life. She watched
her mother hug her sons. She watched Zack
embrace his long lost brothers.

The crowd had been silent while Felix
Martinez spoke. Then the lights came back
on. The room was filled with happy
conversations at every table.

Strangely, the last few years of bitter
estrangement seemed never to have
happened. All everybody wanted to do was
catch up on each other's lives. Felix
Martinez did not look fifty years old
anymore. He looked almost like a young
man. He talked about his cranes and the
thirty-story hotel he would soon be working on. Orlando and Manuel talked about
their next gig in Vegas. They joked with
and jostled each other. The bitterness and
the pain seemed to run from the family like

an infection from a deadly wound. The family was healing.

As they walked from Hortencia's late that night, Naomi, Zack, and their mother hung back. Ahead of them Felix Martinez walked, Orlando at one side, Manny on the other. Their arms were around each other.

"Wait'll you get to the house and meet Brutus," Dad told them. He was laughing as Naomi had not heard him laugh in years.

All was forgiven.